# The Golden Gandhi Statue from America

*Early Stories*



Subimal Misra

*Translated by*
V. Ramaswamy

HARPER**PERENNIAL**

NEW YORK • LONDON • TORONTO • SYDNEY • NEW DELHI • AUCKLAND

HARPER PERENNIAL

First Published in India in 2010 by Harper Perennial
An imprint of HarperCollins *Publishers*

Building 10, Tower A, 4th Floor, DLF Cyber City, Phase II,
Gurugram Haryana – 122002, India

www.harpercollins.co.in



2 4 6 8 10 9 7 5 3

P-ISBN: 978-81-7223-932-9
E-ISBN: 978-93-5029-238-9



Typeset in 11/14.5 Aldine401 BT
Mindways Design Pvt. Ltd.

Printed and bound at
MicroPrints India, New Delhi

# The Golden Gandhi Statue from America
## *Early Stories*

'An iconoclast in his own way, **Subimal Misra** is the living example of a committed writer. Till date, in spite of numerous offers, he has not written a single word beyond little magazines. While many early rebels dwindled in front of money and success, Subimal... represents a vanguard of the literary movement as opposed to the mainstream. Public curiosity about him and media's indifference to him, both leave him totally unperturbed. In Bengal, he can be regarded as the father of the experimental novel – in its widest range. Although numerous articles and books have been written on him, he downright refuses offers of big-time publishers.'

– *Gentleman*, April 1996

In the seven-hundred-year history of Bengali literature, Subimal Misra is the writer who has experimented the most with form and language. A self-proclaimed disciple of Jean-Luc Godard, he was the first to employ *montage* in Bengali literature, which he did in order to declare rebellion against the myth of the narrative and the age-old tradition of story-telling. Misra has explored newer horizons by bringing in film language into Bengali literature. He has made William Burroughs's *cut* method his own, sharpening it to make it more effective. From Brecht, he learnt class consciousness and hatred of class, and from Sartre, the honesty and courage to ignore prizes and praise. Misra considers Vyasa, Proust, Joyce, Kafka, Dostoevsky, Borges, de Sade, Chandidas and Kamal Kumar Majumdar to be his 'soul companions' in creativity. He fiercely attacks middle-class mentality and pillories its values. Misra writes 'with venom instead of ink' in order to make readers cry out in pain, the pain of desolation and helplessness, when the long-nurtured veil of objectivity and hypocrisy is shattered. He examines a single fact from multiple standpoints, using data and reportage, towards portraying civilization with its fangs and wounds. Misra's writing attacks the time, society, oppressors and even himself, and desecrates contemporary myths, dogmas and values. He plays with form, not to befool readers but to reveal the hidden power latent in language. The centrality of language and style in Misra's writing make him difficult to translate.

**V. Ramaswamy** is a Kolkata-based business executive, grass-roots organizer, social planner, teacher and writer.

*To*
*Jean-Luc Godard,*
*who taught me language*

# Contents

# Translator's Acknowledgements

I have been extremely fortunate to benefit from the encouragement, comments and suggestions of many people. Mrinal Bose introduced me to the name of Subimal Misra and prodded me on throughout. Subimal Misra gave me his unstinting approval and trust, without which I could not have proceeded. The late I.K. Shukla also gave the project his blessings. Ankur Saha referred me to his article on Subimal Misra in the Bengali e-zine *Parabaas* and provided continuous encouragement, as did Souva Chattopadhyay, who made valuable critical inputs and suggestions.

Sandip Bandyopadhyay, Amit Basu, Devananda Chatterji, Abhijit Bhattacharjee, Rosinka Chaudhuri, Mark Maclean, Anjan Ghosh, Shuddhabrata Sengupta, Samir Bhattacharya, Soumitra Das, Lorena Gibson, Somnath Sen, Aditya Dutta Roy, Amul Saha, Aromar Revi and Bhashwati – all took the trouble to read my translations and give their comments.

I fondly remember my late aunt, Revathy Gopal, who gave her comments and suggestions. My other aunt, Malathy Sitaram, was also generous with her comments.

Ahmad Saidullah most graciously expressed his appreciation and took pains to suggest various corrections. Nilotpal Roy read through the story translations and wrote a critical evaluation, besides sharing much about Misra's writing with me. Amit Chaudhuri generously affirmed the value and importance of this translation project.

Sam North, editor of Hackwriters.com, carried four of the stories on this literary e-zine. *Gulf Coast*, a literary journal published by the Department of English, University of Houston, published one of the stories.

I am indebted to Ruchir Joshi for recommending publication of the work, and to Karthika V.K. of HarperCollins India for her interest. It was a pleasure to work with Shantanu Ray Chaudhuri and Pradipta Sarkar of HarperCollins India on the publication. Jan Mohammad devoted immense effort and patience to arrive at the cover design.

I would like to express my gratitude and appreciation to everyone, including those whose names I might have missed out inadvertently. Without this collective support, the present work could not have been completed. However, I remain fully responsible for the final output.

Finally, I would like to acknowledge my debt to my wife, Rajashi, and my sons, Rituraj and Rishiraj, for their patient acceptance of my translational immersion.

V. Ramaswamy

# Preface: My Sansness

These stories were written during the late 1960s and early 1970s, a time to cultivate the pen. At that time, I had merely ventured to explore how to employ, and how far one could employ, chiefly, the montage technique of Sergei Eisenstein in a narrative. From two or three sentences arranged sequentially, one after another, a third sense would emerge; coming out like a spark, it would hit at the readers' aesthetic sense, and haunt their cerebral entity, if they have any; some other meaning would thus be miraculously born. I do not know how far all this has been retained here in these translations.

Ramaswamy has selected the relatively reader-friendly stories, translated them and even arranged to have the collection published. Thanks to his sincerity! What I wish to mention very specifically here to the readers of this book is that those of my writings for which I am regarded as a controversial author, an anti-establishment author, someone establishments are afraid of and stay far away from, are entirely absent here. These are neither the 'anti-stories' written by me during a certain phase of my life, nor am I sure whether any trace at all is to be found here of the tiresome yet tireless sojourn of my ganglionic pen till date, from 'samizdat' via 'tamizdat' to 'magnitizdat', and since 'blue blouse' through 'aleatoric' unto 'degree zero'.

I had once written: 'The bloodier the Naxalite movement in West Bengal grows, Vidyasagar's visage gets chopped off again and again, and the more the pavements of Kolkata become infested with sex-magazines.' During that period, I voluntarily went to teach in a place adjacent to Sonagachhi (Ahiritola), which is the largest red-light zone in Kolkata, and was also one of the dens of the Naxalites. There I was fortunate to observe, from the closest probable proximity, those women as well as their children. I do not know whether or not any impact of any of this has at all been reflected here in these stories!

In the forty-two-year span of my writing life, I have never allowed myself to print even a single letter in any daily or journal of any establishment. I have always kept myself away from all sorts of media propaganda (such as TV shows, radio broadcasts, etc.), felicitation meetings or award ceremonies (whether invited or not). And they have also remained wholly allergic to me, never risking to review any of my books throughout my entire writing life. They do not even mention my name anywhere in their papers. I am entirely an author of and exclusively for the Bengali little magazines. In the most ordinary sense, the little magazine in the Bengali language (nearly 2,200 in number) is, parallel to the establishments, a literary flow that publishes the writings of authors, keeping intact their liberty, and honouring their individuality. All the off-the-beaten-track writing in the Bengali language is published chiefly in little magazines. But the number of true little magazines (in the purest sense of the term) that have some distinguished characteristic values has lately come down to almost zero. Even here, my stand is a bit awkward: I am not a parallel writer of the establishments; rather, my writing is reactionarily counter-establishment. I do want to write, I have written, and am still writing, such pieces which even the little magazines would shudder to publish, and which the establishments will never even dare to touch. I have very distinctly conveyed in black and white that I am frightened that success might come; if it comes during my lifetime, I would think that whatever I have written is not very novel.

The stories compiled here are no more than merely samples of my maiden and earliest literary practice. The readers can do fair justice to these stories only if they consider this to be simply a staircase, ascending which one may further comprehend the latter phases of my writing.

Subimal Misra
*February 2010*

# The Golden Gandhi Statue from America

Haran Majhi's widow had no option. Slung a rope round her neck and died. The bloated corpse of the twenty-two-year old floated down the turbid waters of the creek. Two crows had cawed for a long time, now they would go back.

Enter a one-and-a-half-year-old boy: dark, skinny, with a badly distended spleen; whimpering, panting. A cow chewed grass beside the sheora fencing. Two old fogies expressed sadness at the boy's misfortune. After this, they would discuss the lack of character of the wife.

'The wife's twenty-two-year old, firm body… many fond desires in her heart, oh dear… nothing fulfilled.'

'Haran Majhi was an animal. If she ever returned late from the brahmin hamlet after selling muri, he would beat her up… beat the poor thing half-dead.'

The corpse floated down towards Kalighat. The crows following became weary. On the two sides of the creek, a wonderful sight: people had defecated near the water; a stupa-like heap of the world's garbage; sack slung on shoulder, a female rag-picker collecting paper; three buffaloes, their bodies immersed in the foul water, motionless. A dead, decomposed dog, cat, or something like that, floated by – on that too, a crow. People came to Kalighat, bathed in this water and washed away their sins. Who knows how far away Haran Majhi's wife's dead body was. It floated towards Kalighat.

Haran Majhi had left the wife orphaned, as the wife now left the child. 'There's no sin in the child's body, a child is like god; pick it up, take it and go, you'll be blessed,' said someone loudly.

After Haran Majhi died, his widowed wife sold muri to feed herself and her child. Many educated people lived in the brahmin hamlet. They tended rajanigandha gardens in front of their houses, wore new clothes during Durga puja and threw money and coins to the monkey-man after watching the monkeys perform. Observing Haran's wife's firm body, they wanted to keep her as a paddy-husker.

Seeing the crying child, someone picked it up and held it – the drool of the mouth and mucus from the running nose had choked it – before furtively putting it down on the ground.

At the time of her entrance into the earth, Sita had said: 'Oh Mother Earth, split open, give me shelter in your bosom.'

'The responsibility for the stomach is a great burden, kid. You lot won't fathom why the wife went astray,' some people from within the crowd muttered.

A demon's strength in Haran Majhi's wife body, she stood like the ogress Putana at the entrance of Writers' Building, tree-club in hand! People were paralysed by fear! Many, standing and seeing the situation was grave, began to wonder whether tickets would be available for the matinee show at Metro Cinema.

Weevils finally infested Haran Majhi's plough. Of course, many did say it wasn't weevils but termites that destroyed it. Because Haran Majhi had no land, he was a share-cropper on the land of the big landlords of the brahmin hamlet. With the introduction of the practice of recording share-croppers, they did not entrust Haran with their land again.

All India Radio had just announced that hungry people in procession advanced at a speed of one-hundred and eighty-six thousand miles per second.

Haran Majhi's widow saw the entire nether region of darkness before putting a rope to her neck. Someone laid snares and caught birds. As a large raven called out – *ka-ka* – and flew away, the place became a dry desert.

When the Tartars travelled through the desert and the water was spent, and they were close to death with thirst, they killed their own camel and tried to quench their thirst with its blood.

On the boundary ridge sat the peasant's son, merrily eating cold, stale rice with roasted chilli. Before him was a green thicket; he would stay in the hollow beneath that. A slight distance from there, the creek, on whose waters Haran Majhi's wife's dead body floated. And this creek flowed a great distance, went through Tollygunge and touched Kalighat.

There was a lot of commotion at the meeting about the coming elections that had been organized in front of the monument in the Maidan. Trams and buses were set on fire, and the statue of Mahatma Gandhi which stood at the intersection of Park Street and Chowringhee was somehow broken. While everyone lamented saying 'Oh lord, what a terrible thing has happened!' America announced they would pay for a golden Gandhi to be made and put up there!

The wife's necklace, her last consolation. Haran had broken down and wept as he went to sell this precious possession. Of course, even the crows of the world didn't have a clue that he had wept. 'Widowed women's fasting stomachs are the most auspicious places for laying babies… When the shitfuckers can't wait any longer and take off their clothes and poke the crotch, one doesn't remember that nothing's gone to the stomach the whole day, that the belly is hollow. Even being born a dog would have been better than this – oh, how hateful a woman's life is…'

Haran Majhi used to say, 'Sons of whores, just don't let one eat and get by anyhow.' A few months after that, Haran died. Carrying his plough to the land, an altercation with the landlord, and that eventually culminated in bloodshed. Blood's thinner than water. Head split in two, crimson blood gushing out, Haran had come to the veranda and fallen unconscious. He never regained consciousness. Haran Majhi's wife, her child in her arms, stood rooted to the ground and gazed at the sight: the big, stout man rendered lifeless.

In Writers' Building, there was a commotion. The precise reason why Haran Majhi's wife committed suicide had not yet been found. According to the government's calculations, this year, the state of West Bengal had a food-grain surplus! India's prime minister said in a speech, 'We won't let even a single person of our country die stricken by famine… that is, of starvation…' Some people said: 'Rats eat up most of our food grains. If we could just eliminate the rat species, we'd be free of anxiety.'

A few jackals dragged Haran Majhi's wife's corpse to the bank. Tearing the stomach, they found a live baby inside. In a flash the baby rose up to the sky and shouted out:

*The one who will vanquish you is thriving in Gokul!*

All over India, people heard this voice, but couldn't understand who the 'you' referred to.

'Golden statue of Gandhi from America to arrive in this nation very soon!' newspapers reported in big, bold headlines.

Western social scientists had undertaken epoch-making research, proving that people of the modern age were exceedingly chaste. Haran Majhi's widow used to say: 'The old fogy brahmin bastards give a few morsels to eat, and, day or night, only want to squeeze. You bastards will be mongrels in hell in the next life!'

There was a terrible furore everywhere! In the evening, the old landlord from the brahmin hamlet was about to enter his house for his evening prayers after washing his hands and feet at the pond bank, wooden slippers on his feet, when he trod on something soft. He brought a lamp and saw: Haran Majhi's wife's corpse! 'Lord almighty! The whore slept with all and sundry and swelled her stomach and finally popped it in the veranda of a brahmin's house!' The city's mayor got up to go to the bathroom, it was two in the morning. As he entered, he smelt a terrible, foul odour near the door. He turned on the light and saw Haran Majhi's wife's corpse lying there! A renowned people's leader, who was busy the whole day with various kinds of social service, just as he was about to sit at the dining table in the afternoon – a stench. Haran Majhi's wife's corpse lay on the table! At dawn, as the tram driver drove the tram, he suddenly pressed a handkerchief to his nose and with exploding eyes saw the road ahead blocked. Haran Majhi's wife's corpse lay on the road!

The news spread throughout the city. Everyone moved around with frightened, dead-fish eyes. Under the seats in the rooms of the honourable folk… behind cupboards… on the floor of the dining room… in the darkness of the bathroom… Haran Majhi's wife's corpse was discovered!

The one-and-a-half-year-old destitute child cried away in some unknown woman's bosom. The news reported that the golden Gandhi statue from America had set off for Dum Dum! Innumerable crows and vultures could be seen flying around in the sky. The citizens moved about with handkerchiefs constantly pressed to their faces. Stench pervaded the whole city. Everyone was in panic and terror. Who knew when, who, was going to fall into the clutches of Haran Majhi's wife's corpse!

On people's lips now there was only talk of Haran Majhi's widow's corpse. In the morning, the American plane landed at Dum Dum. In every direction, all the honourable people waited. A reverential moment: the golden statue of

Gandhiji was on this plane! From within the crowd it was heard: 'Gandhi is our ideal! We venerate Gandhi.' The one-and-a-half-year-old orphan child kept crying. Someone raised his hand and pointed to the crows and vultures flying in the sky.

Now the wooden box was lowered, the lid was about to be opened. Our national leader extended his gloved hand to touch the golden statue of Gandhiji. The military stood in attention in state honour. The national flag of silk fluttered. Drums played to a steady beat. Many useless people craned to see what was up from afar. They were not allowed to approach.

The lid of the box was opened and, immediately, the entire mass of people present saw, to their amazement, Haran Majhi's wife's decomposing corpse right on top! The whole assembly was shocked. They put handkerchiefs to their noses and realized that unless Haran Majhi's wife's corpse was removed, they wouldn't be able to reach the golden statue of Gandhi.

*1969*

# Uncle Seer

Uncle Seer lived in the grove's horse-neem tree. Everyone in the neighbourhood knew him, young and old, men and women. But no one could say exactly where he came from. When the whole region was redolent with the fragrance of neem flowers in the flowering season, Uncle Seer would sit on the highest branch, legs dangling, and say: 'Tell me, kids, what's the difference between the smell of flowers and the smell of shit?' The boys did not understand; they thought it was a big joke, giggled – *hee hee!* – and ran away.

Uncle Seer's big grievance was why humans did not move around on all fours, lizard-like. 'It's what's best for humans,' he said. When golden moonlight fell on the bamboo grove, he descended from the horse-neem tree and somersaulted around. With his tongue he licked the cool feeling of that array of golden leaves. Beside the bamboo grove was a pond in which frogs floated about. Walking on all fours, Uncle Seer would descend into the water. When he emerged, his body covered in mud and slime, and walked about with his chest puffed out, he really looked like some gigantic, prehistoric reptile.

Uncle Seer used to say: 'All the bastards are intent on hole-poling!' When he said this and loudly smacked his thigh – *thop! thop!* – people laughed. They said: 'Understood the hole's the currency coin with a hole, but what's poling? *Hee hee hee*!' Uncle Seer got mad and said, 'You don't believe me, you luckless wretches!' Then, catching someone by the neck, he chanted the spell 'Om kling kling, burst on the wife, shaha!' and became clairvoyant. He saw that Mr Chief Rent Collector entered his widowed sister-in-law's room on tiptoe; anonymous rats furtively ate away the grain in the granary of Mr Chowdhury, the owner of a thousand acres of land; the boy who won a scholarship in the matriculate examination woke up at dawn to prepare for his coming exams and sang Ramprosad's devotional song, 'Mother, make me your trustee…' After that, he released the fellow's neck and said, 'Pay, you bastard, pay! Give two pennies and go… you've seen a lot!'

Everyone feared Uncle Seer because of all these chants and spells, and no one dared to annoy him. People fondly brought him green bananas and radishes from the fields. Uncle Seer sat on the branch of the horse-neem and chewed and ate them raw. The piece of cloth he wore often hung from the trunk of the tree. The village maidens passing by who suddenly caught Uncle Seer like this turned their faces away and exclaimed, 'O ma!' Uncle Seer said, 'Whatever they might say, they're enjoying it for sure!'

Once, something like this happened. Mr Chowdhury's elder son-in-law, accompanied by his wife, came on a visit from Calcutta. Early in the morning one day, he was out on a walk with his wife when he suddenly saw Uncle Seer sitting naked on the treetop. Seeing him, Uncle Seer laughed – *hee hee!* – and said, 'Charming maiden, your wife!' The modern-minded youth could not tolerate such vulgar behaviour. He gathered people there and brought Uncle Seer down from the tree. What a hiding! One would have thought that his bones had been smashed. But as it turned out, after the thrashing, he shook himself and stood up. Saying 'But what I said was true', Uncle Seer laughed his way back to the top of the horse-neem.

No one really knew what Uncle Seer did in the dead of night, or where he went. Some said he could be seen walking about on all fours in the darkness. Some said he meditated on death in the cremation-ground. If he was ever asked, he would say: 'I go to see the rats eating up all the grain of the country. I go to see how on moonlit nights the moon in the sky becomes dishevelled like a comely young widow…' Hearing such talk, people lost their inclination to enquire and went away. Uncle Seer hurled his laughter – *hee hee!* – after them.

This was the kind of person Uncle Seer was, and his final few days were quite extraordinary. Cholera visited the village. Even the old folk had never seen the likes of such an outbreak. First it hit the hamlet of the fisher-folk. Bishu, a young fisherman, ate his rice at noon and left to catch fish. When he returned, he had loose bowels, vomited a few times and then turned cold. After a couple of hours, Bishu's wife had watery motions. In no time at all, the disease spread throughout the fisher-folk's hamlet. In the first night, nine deaths were reported. In the morning, the sickness moved to the brahmin hamlet. Everyone was terrified, no one could figure out what they should do. By noon, with five corpses being removed from the brahmin hamlet, people fled the village. They went wherever they could. No time to look at wife or son or father. Everyone was anxious to save his own life. Towards evening, vomiting and watery motions hit the kayet hamlet as well. The few brave folk who remained in the neighbourhood, who showed their courage by not leaving, now began to move out on various pretexts. Monoroma, wife of a young man, Gour Mondol, emptied her bowels a couple of times and collapsed in the veranda. The pupils of her eye became lifeless, like those of dead fish. Gour's father said, 'Gour, if you want to save your life, come on, let's run now.' Gour looked once in his wife's direction. He was very attached to his wife; her body still had the ripe fullness of youth. Understanding the son's mental state, the father said: 'If one wife goes, there'll be another, but if life goes once…' Gour submitted obediently to his father's dictum. Probably intuiting the situation, the wife said something like, 'Take me along, don't leave me behind I pray… I fall at your feet!' She rushed towards the street and fell unconscious again. She fell beneath the horse-neem. Uncle Seer sat atop the tree. Observing the wife's plight, he climbed down. He pressed and examined her hands and feet, looked at the pupils of her eyes, and realized that, with care, she could be saved. A few people were walking by the place. He called out to them, saying, 'Help the girl, she might survive.' But they ran away from afar, avoiding treading close to even the shadow of the tree. Uncle Seer looked; gazing, he inhaled deeply.

After that, he thought awhile, said 'vyom tara' and sat down on his haunches near the girl. He loosened the cloth around her waist. The cloth was smeared with shit. He wiped the vomit frothed around her mouth. He brought water and washed and cleaned her and tried to revive her. After quite a few hours of effort, the girl came to her senses. Uncle Seer was then applying a compress to her arms and legs. Becoming aware that she was lying naked in front of a man, the girl almost died of shame. Uncle Seer told her, 'What's the shame, ma? I'm like your son, I serve you.'

Thereafter, when the girl was fully restored to health, Uncle Seer did something calamitous. He went up close to the girl and said, 'I desire you.'

Stunned, the girl said, 'What?'

Uncle Seer said, 'I seek sexual favour.'

The girl nearly died of shame.

Uncle Seer said:

*If a good turn's done, without asking a price,*
*It's either a lie or an artful device.*

The girl did not have a clue what to do.

Uncle Seer held her hand lovingly and said:

*'Twixt mother and wife, discriminate not a whit,*
*One bestows milk and the other a tit!*

Uttering this, he gently rustled the cloth covering her bosom.

When the people of the village heard about this, they became terribly enraged with Uncle Seer. They said they would not tolerate such moral turpitude. First, a person of character threw a potsherd in Uncle Seer's direction. The second person of character threw a stone. The third person of character a hard piece of earth. And the fourth person of character a whole brick. The brick hit Uncle Seer right in the middle of his head and he fell to the ground from the horse-neem branch. Now the assembled people of character began beating him unconscious. But he was still smiling, and the blood from his forehead ran down his face and formed a bloody smile on his lips. That assembly of people of character beat Uncle Seer until he was senseless. They kicked him around like a ball and finally threw him into the river outside the village. To the end, the bloody smile remained on Uncle Seer lips.

The next day all the chaste people of the village saw that horse-neem saplings had sprouted wherever Uncle Seer's blood fell. The tender leaves of all the neems trembled in the morning's bright light and fresh air.

*1969*

# The Camel

I dream every night. I don't like it at all if I don't dream. When I can't, the next day feels utterly empty. I feel hollow inside. I roam the streets all day long. After dreaming again at night – I am at peace.

All my dreams are strange. Sometimes, I dream I'm gnawing and gorging on human bones. Fresh, warm blood trickles down the two sides of my mouth. Slung around my waist is a golden stone, the heel bone firmly gripped in my hands. I chew away at the bone to my heart's content. With practised ease I eat, my eyes shut. As I feed, it strikes me that I've been gnawing away at these bones for ages on end and yet my hunger does not subside. As soon as I realize this, I am filled with grief. To take my mind off that sorrow I try fiddling with the golden stone slung around my waist.

At other times, I dream my face has changed. No one can recognize me. Acquaintances pass me by when I am near. In those dreams, my eyes burst with tears. I feel humiliated by my friends and relatives.

Sometimes, I dream I'm blind in one eye. Lame. Face covered with pock-marks. I wear a dirty shirt over a lungi. I limp around at the bus-stop, staff in hand. I beg people for money. My eight-year-old daughter accompanies me. People treat with me pity. Or they are disdainful.

Every now and then, I have a nice dream. I see a little stream, a tiny dinghy on it. I'm sitting in it. The tide comes in. The waves splash against the banks. The boat rocks and sways. I rock too. The water, the boat, the little waves, all rocking forever, *dol dol duluni*...

Sometimes, I see that I've climbed to the top of a tall building. From there, the people below appear midget-like. How tiny the buses, the trams and the roads have all become! I see them from an entirely different perspective. I really enjoy this dream. This one is quite different from the ones I usually have. That's why I like such dreams.

But some dreams terrify me. I might dream that there's been a conspiracy whereby all my organs and body parts are removed and all kinds of other things are stuffed in their place. These dreams seem to go on forever. I dream that plans are afoot to somehow transform me overnight. The exterior remains unchanged. Only all the inner organs are removed. I really dread such dreams. My whole body turns icy in terror.

When I awaken, I stay lying in bed for a long time. I press and feel my joints and ribs. I feel as if someone has indeed metamorphosed my inner parts. Standing in front of the mirror, I examine my face. A kind of suspicion seizes me. I go out to the street. My mind is constantly crowded with gruesome thoughts. I can't think about anything else even for a moment. Cigarettes feel tasteless. I don't feel like looking at the women on the street. I don't like reading the newspaper. I have no enthusiasm to shave. I don't go to work. I just roam the streets, the sun beating down on my head. When I spot friends, I hurriedly cross the street to the other pavement. Roaming around thus all day, legs weary, I return home in the evening and lie waiting in bed for a nice dream.

But it's very hard to have a nice dream. After all this time, having dreamt so many dreams, I've realized it's not easy to dream a pleasant one. Yet I lie waiting in bed for at least a passable kind of dream. But the worst dreams crowd into my head. The dream where I'm munching human bones appears. The changed-face dream comes. I dream I've become the blind, lame, pock-marked beggar. I lie in bed, sometimes motionless, sometimes restless. Sometimes, I try my best to think about something else. But nothing ever works.

The sounds of railway shunting from the station far away float by. The clock tower strikes – *dong! dong!* – at two, three at night. The eerie silence of night collects and gathers around me. I lie there, eyes shut. Sometimes, I open my eyes.

Motionless darkness surrounds me. Cockroaches walk over my arms. Rats scurry around near me. A few crows wait to peck out my eyes. My body begins to decompose in the sun's sweltering heat and raw darkness. And crows, jackals and vultures wait nearby to tear, dig into and devour it. I see vultures circling in the sky above, casting their shadows on my body. I see a crow staring at me from the stump of a dead tree. A pack of jackals lie in wait for the kill. Their teeth are sharp, the taste of fetid blood on their tongues.

Everything goes haywire! I feel nauseous. Nevertheless, I still wait for a nice dream. I pour out water from the earthen pitcher and drink. From out of the darkness, a maroon flower and the golden stone simultaneously float into view. The bloody fragrance of the maroon flower emanates from my lower limbs. My reflection appears on the golden stone. A half-eaten skeleton of a horse is laid on my right side.

A camel advances, crossing a river. A naked woman sits astride that camel. My mouth turns dry at the sight. No sound escapes my lungs. I study the camel's ashen colour minutely, its ugly, large belly, its curved neck, hump and face. I try to identify the woman's face. But I fail to recognize her. I see only her bare, golden legs dangling on either side of the camel.

The grey camel treads the water of the southern river and advances steadily towards me, the nude woman on its back. Like a spill of blood, the maroon flower petals float away into the distance in the stream's water. The golden stone turns pale. On the dead tree stump nearby, the fiendish crow lies in wait. The vultures circle the sky, casting their shadows on my body. My body rots in the heat of the sun. I try to reach out and cling to whatever I can, but my arms are paralysed. I try to leave everything and escape. But my legs won't move. Lying helpless, utterly bereft, I wait for some good to befall me. But my eyes burst with tears. My face drifts away in the tears and, in a trice, the water rains down on this rocky earth. My heart is heavy with grief.

Like inevitable fate, treading steadily, the camel crosses the river and advances towards me. On its back, the unclothed woman. The woman's face is unrecognizable, blurred. I see only her lovely golden legs and the camel's ashen belly. Its long legs are knee-deep in the mountain stream's clear water. It tramps over yellow flowers and green vines.

The heat is stifling. Sunlight and darkness accumulate together. The crows and vultures fix their sight on their target. Close to my left ear, a very loud cry – *ka! ka!*. On my right side, the half-eaten horse's skeleton lies conspicuously.

The grey camel advances with the nude woman on its back. It crosses the river in the south. I can hear the tread of its hooves. I see its unmoving eyes. The crows, jackals and vultures all call out in unison. The shadows of the three creatures troop in procession across my body. The sunlight and the heat hasten its decomposition. The maroon flowers become invisible in the distant stream. The golden stone turns ashen.

I am enveloped in silence. No more tears flow out of my eyes. All my grief and sorrow reach a point that is beyond disquiet. There's nothing for me to see, nothing more to think about. In vain have I waited here, under this sun, for some pleasant dream.

*1972*

# The Bird

Bhutu wanted to go fishing right away. He wanted a fishing rod, some bait and a river, or least a medium-sized pond. But where would he get a fishing rod or bait, and where on earth a river or pond! Everyone tried to explain to him: 'Listen, Bhutu, don't be like that. Come on, let's all of us go and watch the flight of birds.'

They had to wend their way through villages, where there was greenery, dense thickets and the fragrance of dry earth wetted with rain. Naked boys with their fingers stuck inside their mouths cavorted around, their eyes as big as fish. Bhutu wanted to go and hug them. Ghomta-drawn village women hurriedly moved aside seeing the band of men. Bhutu wanted to hail them and ask: 'Which village are you from, o maiden?' But nothing could be said and nothing known. That band, Bhutu and company, simply passed them by. They were going to see the flight of birds.

It was late afternoon. They reached an empty field and halted. Rail tracks. Straight lines laid out, parallelogram-like, across the field, as far as the eye could see. Some people went up to the rail embankment. Some put their ears to the telegraph posts to hear. Climbing up to the rail track, Bhutu cast his eyes all around. Picking up a stone and flinging it far away, he asked, 'Birds? Where are the birds? Where will we see them flying?' Everyone looked up to the dark clouds in the sky, but there weren't any birds there. Not a single one. They were speechless with astonishment. They had believed that wherever there were rail tracks, there would be birds – they would sit clinging to the telegraph wires. Several of them had spotted tattered feathers by the rail tracks, as well as bits of dried-up bird remains. But there were no birds today. Fatigue was writ large on their faces. In the light of the setting sun, their shoulders stooped, they were a shadow of themselves. No, no birds here. Not a single one to be seen in flight.

Bhutu muttered to himself: 'All this... it's a shame to leave all this behind.' They could go hunting if they stayed. Could find a fishing boat, bait and a river, or, if nothing else, at least a medium-sized pond. But here, on this elevated rail track, there was only the late afternoon sun. Picking up some stones, Bhutu flung them here and there. He felt like doing something really nasty.

A couple of them mustered up courage and went up to him. They said, 'Yes, of course! We'll find the birds. If we go further south, there's a dry river bed. There's a broken bridge there, an ancient one. Its hollows are simply decked with birds. Lots of people have seen it in their childhood. We could go there to see the flight of birds.'

Bhutu grumbled. 'You just said they'd be at the rail tracks. And now you say we have to go south. I just can't understand what you lot are up to!'

The group decided to go south. Their eyes and faces were filled with a sense of unease. The sun's rays shone from their right to their left. Every now and then, there was the sound of stones being flung. Tired, their heads bowed, they advanced. As they advanced, they stooped.

Bhutu didn't want to walk any more. Yet he remained hopeful. A black calf stood near the rail line, a bell on its neck, its eyes hapless. It bleated. A buffalo chewed grass under the acacia tree. The sight brought alive lots of memories for Bhutu. This black calf, its bell, this buffalo – why, he knew them intimately! He wanted to reach out and touch, but he didn't. He just kept his heart's ache inside his heart. As they walked along, he saw a naked fisher-boy walking by, carrying a shapla-vine. His dripping, oiled body glistened in the sunlight. Paddy-gathering women returned home from gathering, walking dignifiedly with their bundles of grain-stalks. Bhutu badly wanted to ask the fisher-boy for a shapla flower. He wanted to laugh and chat a while with the paddy-gathering women. But nothing was said and nothing done. They walked on. Bhutu just kept his heart's ache within his heart. He merely picked up a few stones and flung them here and there.

And so they advanced. After some time, they reached the old bridge. There were gaping cavities among the ruins of the bridge, the red brickwork exposed in abandonment. They looked around, but could not spot a single bird. Someone or the other had come here as a child and seen birds. But there were no birds here now. They had all disappeared somewhere.

Everyone in the group was crestfallen. All of them were tired and dejected. They sat down beside the rail line and tried to think. No one said anything. Bhutu thought it would have been better if they hadn't come out like this to see the flight of birds. Would have been better if they'd tried to find a fishing rod, bait and a river and gone fishing instead. He saw the setting sun's light die in front of his eyes. Some people enthusiastically picked up the fallen feathers from here and there. 'There definitely used to be birds here. Here's proof.' Bhutu fluttered the feathers. Everything inside him changed. He lifted his face and looked in the direction of the rail line. He looked at the broken bridge below and the dry riverbed beneath the bridge. There was water once in this river. There were birds here. But not any more. Someone said, 'The bird-hunters have killed all the birds.' Another said, 'No, there are forests further south. There's a river there, there's a lot of greenery there. The birds have flown there.'

Bhutu didn't like all this. It would have been better not to have come here, only to feel so sad. It would have been fantastic if they'd found fishing gear and bait and a river and gone angling instead. His head was filled with old memories. He hadn't hugged the naked boy they had passed by. He hadn't asked the ghomta-drawn women where their father's home was. He hadn't touched and felt the black calf with the bell. Sadness filled his heart. It grew. Unable to bear it any more, Bhutu stood up.

Bhutu stood and looked at the rail line, at the steel tracks. The last rays of the setting sun had left the sky. Darkness had descended all around. In that semi-darkness, Bhutu was filled with a desire to find a lot of things. He wished he could search once more in the dark hollows of the broken bridge for the clay doll he had lost as a child. He was sure he had lost the doll here, in this very darkness. Trusting his weight upon the broken, whittled-away bridge, he descended. His mind was filled with a host of memories from times past. The others continued to sit beside the rail line. They cautioned him: 'Don't go down there, its dangerous.' But he couldn't hear their warnings. He climbed down, descending step by step. He thought he would surely find the lost doll of his childhood among the hollows of the ancient bridge's ruins.

Descending from the suspended bridge, Bhutu stepped on the ground below. The earth was still soft. There was water here not so long ago. He touched the dry moss on the bridge. He put his hand to his nose to smell the fragrance. A kind of cold, moist, earthy smell. He thought that if he searched around like this for a while, he would surely find his lost doll. Walking sure-footedly, he went deeper and deeper into the semi-darkness. More dense darkness there. He held on to the moss-covered wooden bridge and advanced. The others called out from above, 'Don't be stupid, Bhutu! Come back! It's dangerous there!' But their warnings didn't reach his ears. He carried on, entering into greater darkness. He kept searching. Suddenly, his ankle hit something hard. He thought he'd found the lost doll of his childhood. He picked up the object and brought it to his eyes to recognize it. Even in that impossible darkness he could clearly see that it was a dead bird. Its breast was pierced by steel. As he stroked and gazed at it he recalled he had been a hunter ever since his childhood days. He used to kill birds with small balls. Trembling with excitement, Bhutu realized that it was not steel but a pellet of burnt clay that was embedded in the dead bird's breast.

*1971*

# The Money Tree

Two-and-a-half vulnerable humans reached the shelter of the red light on Park Street after walking long. Pointing excitedly at the red neon advertisement that hung like an icon over their heads, the girl exclaimed to the man, 'Look! Look how it's suck'd up the heart's blood!' The baby began to cry. A spring breeze wafting down from the Maidan floated by, touching the two-and-a-half humans.

On that smooth-surfaced road, they saw a donkey, white in colour, lying dead. That really white donkey, against the black tarmac, four legs splayed high, was visible from far away. But despite seeing it, no one looked at it. The cars skirted it and passed by. The people walked by, handkerchiefs pressed to faces. Those without handkerchiefs held their noses with their fingers and went by that place.

They went close to the donkey. They saw a stream of red blood that had flowed from its ear, wetting the road. Now that had dried up and the blood's colour couldn't be discerned any more. They saw the pupils of the upturned eyes of the donkey. They saw a fly sitting near its belly. The stomach was horribly bloated. They wondered how the donkey came to be here, on this road. But their hunger-crazed minds didn't worry about such things for long.

The man grabbed the infant from the woman's bosom and started begging near the cars that stopped at the red light: 'Babu, just-a-penny!'... The man then had to undertake various acts using his vocal chords and limbs, like hunching up his whole body and bringing his voice to a whining cry, and that utterance had to be relentless because until the 'Babu, just-a-penny!' cry drove the people in the cars to despair, they'd not fling him a coin or two. Sometimes, he would have to hit his empty belly. This circus act was vital to prove that he'd really not eaten, or wasn't being able to eat and, thanks to it, some people would be moved to pity, or assailed by this sound, and throw out some coins.

Apart from doing all this, those two-and-a-half humans also did other things. The woman would lay the baby on the pavement and lie down beside it; the man would shriek and try to grab the attention of the pedestrians: 'Haven't eaten. Here, babu, two-pennies!' Performing all this, on and on, they'd get a few coins. People still indulged in charity in order to achieve pious merit.

Since the evening was advancing, a cool breeze from the Maidan wafted down and passed by, touching them. The baby began whimpering in hunger. The woman pressed the infant to her bosom and gazed blank-eyed at the darkness of the Maidan, at the people on the road, at the trams and buses, at the few youths walking along, looking furtively at her exposed bosom out of the corner of their eyes. She just gazed on.

After a while, their eyes settled upon the white donkey. A few dirty, skinny boys wearing loincloths came and cut out flesh from that dead donkey's carcass. The girl pointed this out to the man and the two of them gaped at that sight. Soon, there was a crowd of greedy humans. All of them came and cut away meat from that carcass, quickly finishing off the white donkey. They too were tempted. They said something like this:

'People're eatin' white donkey's meat!'

'I can see people're eatin!'

'Mussay, white donkey's amazin', dear!'

Jostling and pushing through the crowd, they tried to get in, and once in, they saw the donkey was almost laid bare. They thought: 'We shouldn't delay any more. Everyone's eating it, why not try some ourselves?' They somehow cut off a bit of the leg and came away.

The man took a bite. The woman took a bite. Biting into the white donkey's leg, there was blood around their mouths. They said to each other:

'Kill'd 'n ate crow once!'

'How is it?'

'Hey, it's sweet!'

'Nah, it's bitter!'

'It's bitter then!'

'Nah, sweet!'

'Mussbe sweet, then!'

'What's eaten with the hungry mouth's sweet!'

As the girl, crazed with hunger, chewed and ate the flesh and bones, two people from across the Maidan crept up like foxes. They stopped under a tree and closely observed their behaviour and movements, especially the girl's youthful body. And because they were standing concealed in the relative darkness under the canopy of the tree, one couldn't guess whether they were decent folk or lowly folk, loafers or pimps. Treading warily, they gradually advanced, looked all around, and then gestured to the couple to come towards the darkness.

Though they were somewhat startled at first, eventually they went up to the two men. Their eyes gleaming like foxes, the men studied them. They looked more at the girl. After that, they asked where their village was. They replied. They wanted to know how long they had been beggars. They replied. Then, pausing somewhat, and affecting a cough, they finally asked whether they desired pots and pots of money.

Hearing this, the couple just stared agog. One of the men then lightly patted the girl's bare back and, pointing to the region of darkness in the Maidan, said, 'There's a money tree there! Shake it and it rains down! If you'd like to gather some, come along!'

They were scared. They wanted to, but weren't brave enough. The two men then emboldened them: 'Don't be afraid! You'll come to no harm!... All this money... a money tree!' Seeing that the man and woman were still frightened, the men put up an act in front of the girl: 'All this money! Pots of money! A money tree! And when you've got money, you won't have to beg! You won't have to eat the rotten flesh of a dead donkey! You can eat two square meals a day!'

Going on like this, when the men saw the girl's eyes lit bright with desire, they knew it was time. They thrust the infant into the man's arms, caught hold of the girl's arm and pulled her along. 'Hey boy, you stand here with the baby. I'll show your wife the money tree and be back.' Without waiting for any response, they dragged the girl by her arm into the fold of the darkness. The man simply stared, benumbed, at the dark clump in the Maidan.

Like foxes, the two men swift-footedly reached the centre of the darkness. The girl realized that she was almost entirely enveloped by the darkness. There were so many lights and people all around. She could see all of them, but no one could see her. The men said, 'You ate the white donkey's flesh. There's still some blood on your lips, wipe it off!' And saying this, one of them took out a silk handkerchief from his pocket and wiped her mouth. The girl gazed vacantly. The men cleared their throats and, fluttering their eyelashes and affecting pious demureness, said, 'The money tree is a precious resource! You can't touch it at just any odd time or in just any way you please. You can only touch it when you're entirely bare. Take your sari off, girl!'

The girl just stared at them. She didn't quite understand what was happening. The men then started taking off their clothes. They said, 'Here, look, we're taking it off too!' The girl didn't quite understand what was happening. Then, unable to control themselves any longer, the two men didn't bother about courtesies any more. They tugged at the girl's torn, dirty sari.

The girl was completely naked under that undifferentiated darkness. Of course, she didn't really feel anything, because she had lost all sensation besides hunger. She had long ago lost even the sense of shame at being naked in front of men.

The red neon continued to glow in the heart of the metropolis. The radiance of that colour spread far. Perhaps that glow would light up her face as well. She just stared into the red hue. Maybe she thought about something. Maybe she didn't. Or maybe she didn't think like this.

The southern breeze came and touched her body. The night's chill floated by her uncovered body. Indifferent to everything, she peered into the faces of the two men to find a trace of the money tree.

*1970*

# Times, Bad Times

Waking up, Adri's eyes first go to the tabletop and then to the letter in red print kept there. Mind blank, Adri gazes at it for a long while. Eventually, he realizes how futile it is for him to just gaze at it like this.

Adri then turns his eyes and looks at the calendar. The picture sways in the gentle breeze. Twenty-second of April, 1967, sways. How much time is left now? It must be seven, half past seven. It will begin at nine in the evening – some fourteen hours or so remain. In these fourteen hours, he has to decide about the present – no, not a present, a gift of love.

Want a cigarette! He picks up the cigarette pack with his left hand and lights one. He doesn't feel like getting out of bed just yet. He puffs on the cigarette a few times and blows the smoke out into the room. Isn't everything he values slowly coming to an end – ambition, joy, health, poetry, Ramola...? What remains, other than just this Charminar? He looks at the cigarette and laughs.

Adri laughs away. Holding the cigarette near his ear – there is a kind of hiss of the cigarette burning which he really likes to hear. It also strikes him that it is as if life itself is burning away with the sound.

Adri's eyes stray – here and there. Searching for something all over the room and not finding it, they wander around restlessly. Bright sunlight outside, but he doesn't feel like getting up. Just lying, clinging to the bed. Adri realizes he isn't in good shape nowadays. Long ago, he used to worry about this, not so now. What is the use of worrying unnecessarily about oneself? As long as it runs, let it, after that, one day, pop, die without anyone knowing. No demands from anyone, no dues. But is it really so? Is the world really so bereft for him? Adri tries to take his mind to another subject. Being exposed before oneself is a frightful thing.

The morning advances. Adri is still lying in bed. And as he lies, he keeps thinking. Ramola once said, 'Look, this unworldly attitude of yours towards everything will destroy you.' He didn't think about this so seriously then, now he understands. He realizes how true this is, and how cruel. If someone said that Adri killed himself, it wouldn't be untrue. Yet there wasn't really any reason behind this, it wasn't inevitable.

Lying in bed and thinking – Adri is doing too much of that these days. Simply too much. Why is he winding up his life? Job! So many people can't get jobs – but how many people waste their lives like this? Nobody has all his aspirations fulfilled, that isn't possible either. But no one leaves everything and idles because of that. Didn't Ramola speak about this to him so many times? 'Look, Adri, do something. How much longer can we go on like this?'

He didn't reply to that. Eyes eager, Ramola looked intently at him, waiting for some response. 'Say something, Adri, at least say yes, or no, or anything.' He silently puffed away at a cigarette, and the lengthening shadows of twilight over the waters of the Ganga deepened. He thought about it. Actually, no reply was possible in such matters. He certainly tried. If he didn't get a job, what could he do? If he got a job, he was willing to marry Ramola. But if he didn't, well then, what more could he do? And as far as Ramola was concerned, well, he had never asked her to come close to him – neither did he have a hand in her going away.

Perhaps each day was insufferable for Ramola. He could understand that. She said, 'You're terribly cruel, Adri, stone-hearted, there's no life in you. No compassion, tenderness, love, affection – nothing whatsoever.' Actually, maybe that is the truth. Every human feeling in him has been exhausted, is coming to an end. But what was Adri to do? He didn't blame Ramola either. She had borne a lot. She had waited patiently for him so many times. How many times did Adri fail to keep an appointment? So many times he didn't even speak properly to her because he didn't feel like it. How many times had she waited in front of a cinema hall, looking repeatedly at her watch, and finally crushed the two tickets into a ball and thrown it away angrily and returned home, face smarting, then fallen to her bed and sobbed her heart out?

Meeting him after that, she fiercely asserted her right to demand a proper explanation, she wanted to know. In reply,

Adri merely affected a smile: 'I didn't feel like it, so didn't come.' Adri realizes how such an explanation would have hurt a woman's heart, but he was helpless, he had no option. He could have made up something, but what was the point? Rather, it was as well that Ramola became acquainted with this aspect of his character, which was best for both of them. How long could it continue after that? Adri had realized it wouldn't last much longer like this, it couldn't.

And it didn't. Ramola gradually stopped coming, stopped meeting him and, ultimately, all contact was erased. And after so long, suddenly, yesterday evening, this letter, Ramola's wedding invitation. Adri gazes for a long time at the colourful letter in red print. His mind wanders again and again, but he doesn't want to be exposed in his own eyes. That would be a terrible thing.

It is getting late, must be half past eight or nine, he should get up now. But what is to be achieved by getting up? Adri continues lying and brooding. Would be nice to get a cup of tea! But he is just as fine without it too. Adri lights another cigarette. Actually, this laziness, this lying silently in bed, is his only consolation. Puffing at his cigarette, he sees the spider's web on the wall. The walls of this room haven't been whitewashed in ages. In many places, the plaster has broken away, leaving ugly, gaping holes. But Adri is unable to focus his mind on such things.

His eyes keep darting to yesterday's letter. Has Ramola invited him in order to hurt him? Or just like that? She knows someone in this world called Adrikumar Roy, she has thought it fit to invite him, and so she has. Since yesterday evening, he has been experiencing a great unease, he hasn't slept well at all at night. Adri realizes he isn't being able to deal with this as easily as he should have. Somewhere, something is happening, is about to happen. However much he tries to be indifferent to everything, somehow he isn't quite able to.

All night long, he has had a bizarre dream. A dark-skinned man had signalled to him to come for coffee; he had descended, for a long time, down a stairway, towards some underground chamber. Eventually, they had reached a cold, dark chamber. He and that boy had been drinking coffee. Suddenly, the room was filled with terrible smoke. Adri had tried to escape, but couldn't find the stairs. Smoke everywhere, he was choking in the smoke, and amidst that smoke he had been searching frantically for the stairs. Adri tries to remember the dream. Why did he have such a dream? Did it point to some repressed desire in his subconscious?

The plain truth is that howsoever indifferent he tries to be, he had felt just the opposite in the dream. In his bid to survive, he had been searching frantically, like a madman, for the stairs. Adri doesn't want to think any more. He knows well enough that there will be no way out if he is exposed before himself.

Even though Adri doesn't want to probe such matters too deeply, he does understand a little. Since yesterday, has he been able to be as detached as before? And what is the use of being so? It is best to calmly accept whatever upheaval was coming. Best in the sense that his true self will thus be exposed – and whatever else happened, it is after all a fact that a kind of apathy is at work inside him. Whatever happened, that force will remain at the foundation of everything. So if he thinks about Ramola today... if he sends a specific present for Ramola – he has been so preoccupied since yesterday about precisely what he should give her! So where do matters stand then? Adri shakes himself. Matters don't stand anywhere, it is merely an exception for a day and nothing else.

Puffing on another newly lit cigarette, all of Adri's enthusiasm subsides. He should give something. When she has invited him, reciprocating is a gesture of civility. But to think so much about it – what is there to be so excited about, as he has been since last night? But yes, it is proper to give something, though it should not be like anyone else's gift. Adri is unique in this world; there is only one Adrikumar Roy in this world. If he dies, just this one person alone dies. The gift too should be just as unique.

But he might as well not give anything; it is just as well not to worry about all this. Someone called Ramola – he had known her once, what is there to be civil about? Would anybody point his finger at him and say: 'Despite being invited by Ramola, Adri didn't go?' No one would say that, no one would say anything. The matter is so trivial that he himself would forget about the whole incident in a couple of days. Hence, there is no need to think so much about it.

Now he can lie in bed for a long time without thinking about anything, without worrying about anything. He can stare at the things in the room and smoke any number of cigarettes. But Adri can't remain lying like this for very long. An uneasiness within keeps pricking at him. He puffs at the cigarette and throws it away to the corner of the room. It burns for a while, smoke rises, and finally it extinguishes and becomes a heap of ash.

Adri realizes that it is becoming increasingly difficult for him to find release from all this. It is this lying in bed that leads to all kinds of thoughts crowding in his head. It is much safer to roam around. There would be no specific direction, just wandering around wherever his eyes go.

Despite wanting to get up, Adri idles for some more time. Random images of Ramola's face come to mind. A host of tiny memories crowd his thoughts. Finally, Adri pulls himself up. Outside, the terrible April sun. The rooms of the lodgers who leave for office by ten are locked. Adri goes down the stairs. Where is he going? Lost in thought, Adri descends, turns to the left once to relieve himself and then goes directly to the road outside. He is still wearing the trousers from yesterday, he hasn't changed. His face is unshaven. Adri felt it with his hands but didn't shave. What is the point, what is the point of doing all this?

Coming out onto the road, he sees the sun is beating down. In the lane, kids are playing marbles. There is a bit of shade there. A crow flies down from somewhere and alights on the broken wall, looks this way and that a few times and caws loudly, then flies away. Adri turns the corner and reaches the tramline.

Where is he going, in which direction? He can get by without thinking about that – after all, he is moving in some direction. A tram, crammed with people, passes by, swaying. People hanging from the outside too, so skilfully. A double-decker bus goes by, clouding the whole place with black smoke. At the kerb, the horn of a car is stuck, an old black model. The horn blares unbearably, as if the place is falling apart in that incessant noise. People are crowding around, the public curious. Adri finds it very amusing. The driver is frantically pressing this side and that side of the car – the noise just doesn't stop. The traffic policeman who has been standing at the kerb, umbrella in hand, moves forward. Adri doesn't wait there – heck, don't like it!

He crosses the road. Quite a few people at the bus stop, wearing freshly laundered clothes, anxiously waiting for the bus. The whole world is really so busy, all engrossed in their duties. In their midst, he alone has no work... Amazing! In this wide world, he alone has no important work, he would never have to be busy like them and rush around. Adri feels an ache somewhere. He can see it is good for him in a way. He has no debts in the world, no responsibilities. This wandering around aimlessly, this silent, unperturbed saga... life is just passing by, will come to an end too one day.

But since yesterday, Ramola has been part of his thoughts. Amazing... Ramola is deeply entrenched, despite everything. He hasn't been able to keep thoughts about Ramola at bay. Adri feels quite annoyed now.

Adri feels really helpless then, on that sunny pavement. How like a lifeless puppet he is being assailed by such thoughts! Angrily, Adri searches his pockets for a cigarette. There aren't any. Fortunately, his wallet is in his pocket. The whole of last night, he had felt a mild ache on his left side. Now he realizes he hadn't taken his wallet out last night and it had been under his chest all night. Amazing! Nothing seems to have an impact on him nowadays. Life is moving along just fine.

He stands in front of a paan shop, holds out a few coins and is about to ask for cigarettes when he sees his face floating in the mirror in front. What a sight he is! Whose image is this? Adri is quite unrecognizable. Just as well – what is the point of being in good health, what is the point of being of sound mind, what is the use of worrying about all this? He lights a cigarette and gustily blows a mouthful of smoke towards the mirror. He hears someone calling his name.

Looking around, he sees Abani waving and calling him from across the street. Why Abani now, he would simply bother him... He had been an intimate friend once, how like a stranger he has become now.

He sees how Abani, fatigueless, scampers past the speeding cars like a nimble horse and comes to him. He comes and shakes his shoulder: 'Hey man, what have you done to yourself, can't even recognize you!' Adri observes him, his well-kempt appearance – in the prime of health. Adri wonders why he doesn't feel jealous looking at Abani. Some time back, when Abani hadn't got the job in the bank, how skinny he had been! It is evident he is really happy now.

And with this thought, Adri wonders what it means to be happy. How does one have to be to be considered happy? Isn't he happy? Is he unhappy? He doesn't feel that way. Abani is saying, 'Hey man, why aren't you saying anything? You used to talk a bit before! What's up? Have you stopped even that now?' Adri laughs. Laughing, he greets Abani, says, 'What's happening with you?' As Abani pulls him by his hand, Adri gazes at him. Abani says, 'Come on, let's sit somewhere. Good that we met, need to talk to you.'

After they sit down at a teashop, Abani lights an expensive cigarette and blows out smoke. Adri sees Abani's eyes contracted in pleasure. Offered a cigarette, he too lights up. Looks, sees the folds on Abani's neck, the immaculately shaven face. Abani is saying something. He lifts his face and looks at Abani. He is saying, 'You've remained the vagabond you were, Adri, you don't feel sorrow, don't feel any pain… Do you know Trilochan is now the chief of a top-class firm, a salary of something like two thousand rupees?' Adri laughs: 'That's great!' 'Can you imagine, Adri, this Trilochan once used to beg and smoke bidis from you, and you…'

Adri sees that Abani gapes at his face and stops talking. Abani has realized that it is pointless telling him all this. Amazing! Why does Abani grasp everything so slowly…

'So what's up with you…' Adri has to say something like this. Abani says, 'Nothing at all, pal, still stuck in that branch.' Adri sees that Abani looks frightfully unhappy right now. Abani is not happy with his job. Abani now wants to be Trilochan. But Adri will never want to be like Abani. Adri realizes how it troubled Abani to think about Trilochan. But Adri feels no pain. Adri doesn't want to be Abani. He doesn't want to be Trilochan. He doesn't feel troubled inside, feels no pain. No feelings.

On Abani's order, the waiter comes and hands them two cups of tea, hot tea. Adri watches the smoke rise. So Abani isn't happy either. Robust, brimming with youthful vigour, wonderful, smart clothes, meticulously shaven face, expensive cigarettes – and yet Abani isn't happy. But is *he* happy, or isn't he happy? What does the word 'happy' mean? Adri hears Abani saying something again. He looks at Abani's face. Why is Abani staring at him? What is he looking at? 'Hey pal, what news of Ramola?' Hearing this, Adri realizes that someone has rung a bell inside him, it rings – *ding dong!* So he can't forget about Ramola! A newspaper lies in front. Adri picks it up and begins reading.

After all this time, why Ramola again? Who is Ramola? He doesn't know any Ramola. Adri turns to Abani and laughs. 'Why, what's the matter?' After all this time, why Ramola again? Ramola is just a girl's name, some girl's name, no more than that... Abani is speaking again, saying something: 'Do you know Ramola's marrying a professor?' But what does that matter to Adri? Let a girl called Ramola marry a professor or a businessman, how does that concern him? He should give her a present, that is all, only that much ... Abani wants to say something more. Adri sees that Abani is now feeling sad for him. Like a true friend, Abani feels for him. But nothing in the world matters at all to Adri. Why can't Abani understand this? But yes, this Adri is alone in the world. No good, no bad, no grief, no sorrow, just one responsibility, one duty ahead of him – to send a present of some sort to the wedding festivities tonight.

Having admitted this much, Adri feels relieved. Adri wonders how much more is left to be exposed before him. He looks at Abani who is saying something now: 'You're an amazing chap, Adri, you don't feel the slightest sadness...' Abani stops midway, perhaps he thinks it is futile telling him. Adri feels ill at ease. He pores over the newspaper. A plane crash somewhere, reported in big, bold type. Finance minister's speech... *Plop, ssssss, glug glug.* That's all! Great advertisement: a girl drops a sherbet tablet – *plop* – into a glass of water, with a sound – *ssssss* – the tablet dissolves in the water and makes a sherbet, *glug glug* – the girl drinks it all up. That's all, and all cold! More advertisements... Donate blood at the blood bank to help the sick. Adri's eyes zoom in on that.

Abani is saying something, but nothing registers. Got it, got the present! Adri hadn't imagined it would come to him so easily. He wants to jump up! Giving a gift for Ramola's wedding is no longer a problem for him – he will give her a bottle of blood as a gift, his own blood! He only has to get the blood out of himself, put it into a bottle and then deliver it at the wedding hall. Not a sari, not a pressure cooker, not an iron, nor even a book – but blood, his own fresh, warm blood! What better thing than this could he give Ramola!

Adri realizes he feels a tremendous excitement within himself now, or at least he wants to be excited. It would be something original and elemental, everyone would be stunned! If this had been an earlier time, he would have cut open his breast with a sword and taken out his blood. But times are different now, it is only proper for everything to be in keeping with the times.

Adri is thinking. He can't remain seated there any more. He puts down the newspaper. What is that Abani is saying, what does he want to say? But he can't sit here any longer. 'I'm off, Abani, I need to...' He sees Abani gaping at him in astonishment. He comes out of the teashop.

It is certainly past noon, and he hasn't bathed or eaten. So what, he doesn't like all that. Terribly hot sun. As if the whole world has wilted. Very few people are out on the road now. A fire engine goes by, clanging – *dang dang!* Two people are waiting for a bus at the bus stop. Someone is purposefully setting up his shoe shop on the pavement. He is looking, walking, taking in everything blankly. A ringing inside his head: 'I'll present my own blood for Ramola's marriage, I'll give a blood-gift, blood... blood... blood...'

A fire engine goes by again. All the cars suddenly come to a halt, make way. Some fire nearby, or it could be something else. He walks on. As he walks, he looks, and as he looks, he walks.

Adri is walking along absent-mindedly, in no particular direction, without any aim. Finally, he realizes that his legs ache, his head feels heavy. He feels he has walked for a long time, almost an age. Where has he come to now? Looking around, he sees he has left the tramline far behind, left behind the major thoroughfare. This is probably near the fringe of the city, dust in the air. He wonders why he has come here. Wondering, he looks all around, and then he discovers to his great surprise that he had indeed come a long, long way, and this is the way to Ramola's house!

Standing under the shade of a shop, Adri thinks how, despite being so indifferent, he hasn't been able to get Ramola off his mind. How helpless Adri was before this thing called the mind. He thinks now about giving blood. He thinks about all that he has done since morning. Thinking thus, he realizes nothing is easy, there is no escaping from oneself. Or from one's mind. Overwhelmed, Adri stands there for a long time. He looks extremely helpless and pathetic now, like wan sunlight. He is smoking a cigarette disinterestedly, smoking just for the sake of smoking, standing there as he had nothing to do.

Coming back to his own after that, he calls out to a pedestrian and asks what time it is because he feels he has walked for a very long time and is extremely tired. Hearing the time, he recalls that he hasn't bathed today, hasn't eaten, he has got out of bed and come straightaway out to the road. And it is late afternoon now. After this, the afternoon too would pass, it would be evening, then evening would turn to night, and night to midnight. Yet he would be completely impervious to the passage of time or its untimeliness. He would be standing just like this, or would be walking, or thinking, just thinking and thinking. There would be no end to such thought. The busy world would eventually tire and slump, but Adrikumar Roy would be thinking because Adri's thoughts had neither beginning nor end. With that, Adri stirs somewhat and tells himself he will do something today. He forces himself to think about doing something to get the blood now because it would soon be evening... Meaning, it is time.

A lorry goes by, making a frightful noise; the road ahead is filled with dust. A boy screams his lungs out from a house. The sun falls on the opposite pavement, producing a kind of melancholy colour. Adri, true to habit, feels nothing at all. He just walks on along that pavement in shadow. After a while, suddenly coming upon a doctor's chamber, Adri comes to a halt with a start.

He recalls that he doesn't know much about giving blood, he has merely heard about it. Doctors would surely be able to help him in this regard. Pondering about such things, he pauses for a bit, and then steps right in. Inside, the doctor sits wearing rectangular-frame spectacles. A ray of light from outside seems to be fixed on the lens. Seeing Adri, he nods his rectangular-spectacle-wearing head and says, 'Sit down.'

Adri sits down and is about to explain his predicament, but he sees the doctor trying to examine him. Putting the stethoscope to his chest, pulling up his eyelids, looking at his tongue, his face becomes increasingly grave, and before Adri can say anything, rectangular-face begins speaking: 'Very bad… any fever every now and then?' Adri interrupts the doctor. 'What is the use of worrying unnecessarily about one's health? I am here on an entirely different matter.'

Interrupted, the doctor stares at him. Adri tries as much as he can to explain to the doctor. He needs a bottle of blood – he wants to give his own blood and this should be filled in a bottle, sealed and portable. After explaining everything, he realizes the doctor hasn't grasped it. The doctor is staring in astonishment at his face, gaping at something.

'Blood… I mean… but like this…'

Adri listens, and after trying to explain the whole thing afresh to the doctor, notices that the doctor's forehead is creased, his lips are moving and he is delivering some long sermon in doctor's jargon. Not understanding a thing, Adri gazes on. He looks at the brown tube of the stethoscope lying on the tabletop, he sees 'Dr Probir Roy Choudhury, MBBS' written on the notepad, he sees the curtain of the doctor's chamber swaying in the breeze, he sees the lengthy shadow of the doctor fixed on the wall, and after seeing all this and once again trying to find Dr Probir's eyes behind the spectacles on his brow, he hears the doctor going on again about something. He is about to ask him:

'Doctor…' The doctor is now looking directly at his face and laughing.

The reflected light from his spectacles confuses Adri. The doctor speaks, Adri hears the doctor speaking… 'This can't be done…' Adri makes an effort to speak, he wants to explain that he needs a bottle of blood, it is very important – after all, he wants to give his own blood. In great despair, Adri wants to say all this, he wants to explain he needs it badly.

As the doctor now lowers his face very close to his face, Adri is somewhat embarrassed. The light reflecting like a searchlight from his spectacles searches for his face. 'Are you crazy, mister… how can blood… like this!' Realizing it is hopeless, Adri shoves his hands into the pockets of his trousers, clenches his fists there, opens them, clenches again, opens again, and emerges outside.

Outside, he sees it is a brilliant dusk. What does it matter whether he got the blood or not? He turns his back to the sunlight and walks ahead. Adri can feel the acute weakness in his body. Nowadays, he becomes breathless after just a little effort. So let it be, Adri consoles himself. He won't worry too much about such things, let things be. As long as he is ticking, he will tick on, when it becomes difficult to tick, he will die. The *plop!* sound when a fruit falls from a tree, a gentle sound like that, and then everything will be over. No one to grieve over him, nobody will be concerned.

Shuffling along, Adri now stands over an old abandoned culvert. From there, the station in the distance appears desolate. There is gentle sunlight now on the tin roof of the station and over the houses in the distance. A man swift-footedly crosses the rail tracks and advances towards the station. It will be twilight soon. There is a soft light in the sky and a pleasant breeze is blowing. Adri thinks, surely one train or the other comes to this station sometime in the evening. And so he waits upon that ancient culvert to see the evening train.

*1968*

# The Naked Knife

Butku glanced at his watch. It was two minutes to one o'clock. It was time. He looked this way and that a few times. He then fixed his eyes on the pavement kerb. 'Not a second to waste,' Ghentu had said. He had said, 'Be very careful! Say a thing out of step, and you might arouse suspicion. She's a clever bitch.' And so, accordingly, one had to be very attentive and watchful. Without taking his eyes off his target, Butku took out a cigarette from his pocket and lit it. He let out a lungful of smoke. From the corner of his eye, he once again cast a look at his own body, the pair of black trousers and the flaming red T-shirt. He thought: 'Wow, it's really radiant! Look at it, and your head will spin!' A faint smile formed at the corner of his lips. Flicking away the cigarette, he bent backwards slightly, twisted his torso and stuck his right leg out in front. Meaning, he would stand in that famous film-star's pose. He smirked. Just then, a taxi turned the corner and screeched to a halt.

It took only a couple of seconds for him to spot Mamata and Ghentu seated in the rear, Ghentu's eyes signalling him.

Just as Butku opened the door and got in, the taxi began to move. Mamata was seated in the middle, so when he got in, his leg brushed against hers. Butku saw that Mamata had dolled up wonderfully, the preening bitch. The anchol of her sari kept slipping off her breasts. She looked like a smug tomcat. As Butku tried to put his right hand on her ample rump, the girl pushed it away. 'Damn it!' Butku removed his hand. He saw Ghentu's brows were creased. Meaning, it was not yet time for all this. That meant one had to keep things in check.

The taxi went through the commercial district. A few jolts, body grazing against body. The fragrance of a female body, from her hair and the cheap perfume, pricked Butku's nose. He glanced at Ghentu out of the corner of his eye. He was sitting with his back slanted, positioned as low as possible. Butku remembered they had decided to do just that. Meaning, try to stay as low as possible while in the car, so that it wouldn't be easy for anybody to recognize them. For that might create difficulties. Witnesses and evidence would cause a fix.

Butku lit a cigarette and looked at the people all around. It was now tiffin-time in the offices. A crowd of clerical babus on the street corner ate sliced cucumbers. Many cars were lined up ahead of them. They got stuck too. Looking out, he saw a red-flag procession. He hoped they wouldn't be stuck here for an hour, or even half an hour. But the procession was not such a long one, about mediumish – it shouldn't take long to go by. Butku heaved a sigh of relief and puffed at his cigarette.

The girl, Mamata, fidgeted. She couldn't sit still even for a moment. 'D'you know what I've said at home, Butku-da? That Shanta and Shiuli are going on a holiday and I'm accompanying them.' She laughed – *hee hee!* She looked pretty when she laughed. Butku gaped at her. Ghentu sat motionless, looking tense. He didn't make the slightest movement. A small bag lay beside his feet. All the stuff was inside that, reckoned Butku. The car moved very slowly. The procession didn't advance at all. Butku's exasperation grew. Damn it, who wanted all this now!

Some more time passed. After they had crept along for a while, the road ahead cleared and the car gained speed. They reached Howrah Bridge. Butku saw snatches of the Ganga between the passing girders. The river flowed by, heavily laden boats, steamers and cargo vessels on its bosom. People were busy all around. A heap of cauliflowers. They passed by the orange and apple vendors. The taxi moved along slowly and came to a halt after a while. Ghentu opened the door and stepped out. Mamata couldn't decide which side to get out from. She shifted this way and that, then finally got out. Seeing Ghentu, poker-faced, paying off the cabbie, Butku moved ahead towards the station. Tickets had already been bought. He looked at his watch – there were still twenty minutes to go.

The station was packed with people. The bases of the walls were brown with paan spittle stains. People ran. An announcement: 'Bombay Express running twelve hours late.' A long engine whistle sounded. Butku passed all this by and reached the platform. He looked behind to see if Ghentu and Mamata were coming along all right. Mamata's body brushed against Ghentu's. Her sari was worn well below the navel. A lot of vacant space, like a playfield. Could play football there! She laughed, glowed with her laughter. Ghentu held on to the bag carefully. His face was very grave. Looking at him, one would think of him as a decent, serious youth of few words. The cunning fox could brilliantly conceal his thoughts when, in fact, he had an accomplished master's prowess in netting the catch! Butku slipped as he trod on a banana peel and just about managed to prevent himself from falling.

The train was already on the platform. They ought not to be on the platform where they could be noticed by others. Ghentu signalled with his eyes to get into a vacant compartment. The train was quite empty, but all the compartments had a few people. Butku spotted a small cabin. There was an old woman there – one could make out that she was a villager. She sat crouched, holding a baby girl to her bosom. Butku and company got in there.

Butku didn't do much in the train. It left without anyone else getting into their cabin. It was a splendid late afternoon outside. Winter hadn't arrived, yet there was a slightly chilly breeze blowing. Dust flew in the wind. Butku looked at the old woman. She dozed while the baby girl, her face puckered, gazed outside. Mamata couldn't sit still in one place – she shifted restlessly. The anchol of her sari slipped off her breast, revealing the voluptuousness of her bosom. Oh what a juicy babe! Butku couldn't hold on any longer. Impatiently, all of a sudden, he kissed Mamata's cheek. Ghentu looked her in the eye. Mamata laughed out – *hee hee!* The old woman woke up at the sound of laughter. Not realizing anything, she stared blankly, as did the infant.

Butku had become desperate. He wound his left arm around Mamata's waist. Her bare waist electrified his arm. The old woman stared, as if at something novel, her eyes wide. As he sat like this, Butku twisted a bit to the left and, in a flash, again kissed Mamata's cheek. She almost rolled over with laughter. She moved his hand away. 'Butku, you bastard, if you do this…' – Ghentu's voice. But Butku didn't look in his direction. Ghentu was obviously very angry and sullen now. Bad news. Better not to cross the line. The old woman stared, the baby too.

The train was in motion. At a station, a group of boys, books and notebooks in their hands, got up, shouting and swearing. They got off after two or three stations. All the while, they gaped as one at Mamata's body. An old vendor, a scraggy beard on his chin, shouted for some time: 'Oil for cuts! Tansen pills from Punjab!' Mamata constantly pestered them for things to eat. When a ghugni seller came by, she said she wanted some. She gazed at the moshla-muri. And when she saw lozenges, she wanted even that. Spotting the boiled-egg vendor, she burst out: 'Please buy me one, Ghentu da… I'm terribly hungry!' But no one paid her any heed. Not getting any custom, the egg vendor got off. Mamata's face turned really sad.

The day was coming to an end. The light of the setting sun fell on a fruit-laden orchard. Books referred to such colours as golden. But Butku didn't have anything to do with books or poetry. He didn't like them. The train noisily crossed a bridge. His body rubbed against Mamata's. But

Butku didn't look in that direction. If he looked, he would want to paw.

After getting off the train, a bus had to be taken to reach the sea beach. It had just turned evening when the train stopped. They didn't have any luggage to speak of. Getting off, they crossed the overbridge and boarded a waiting bus. The whole place was enveloped in fog. A solitary lamp shone dimly. Everything looked blurred in that light. Just a few people in the bus, they sat all wrapped up. Some puffed on bidis. The bus sped along. Every once in a while, the headlights showed up hedges and thickets on the two sides of the road. Cycle-rickshaws and, occasionally, like shadows, a couple of bare-bodied villagers floated by. But Butku didn't like looking at all that. There were people in the bus, so it wasn't possible to try any tricks either. Ghentu watched with alert eyes. Ghentu was the most adept and alert one among them. If Ghentu hadn't been there, he wouldn't have been able to carry out this scheme by himself. Hooking Mamata and bringing her out like this would have been impossible on his part, though she was just a girl from the slums and couldn't get enough to eat half the time.

The bus turned a corner with a nasty jerk. It stopped for a bit. People got in or out, and so on. Butku looked at his watch. It was time. In a few minutes, the bus would reach the sea beach. The hotel room had been booked in advance... And after that, the whole night would be hot, hot, hot! He felt a tingling sensation in his lower abdomen, around his crotch. Butku scratched himself.

He wanted to get down to business as soon as they reached the hotel, but Ghentu wouldn't have that. He wanted to take his time doing everything. Butku didn't have much patience. Ghentu looked him in the eye. Meaning, be careful, take it easy.

When the window in the room was opened, the southern breeze entered the room lustily, along with the roar of the sea. The night was dark now, nothing was visible outside. But it was obvious that the sea was nearby, very near. Butku had been here earlier, he had stayed in this very hotel. But he had never ever opened the southern window and gazed at the sea on a moonlit night. He didn't fancy any of that. Gazing at the sea had never held any fascination for him. And the few times he had come here earlier had also been for other business. But Mamata jumped around now, exclaiming: 'The sea! The sea!' Butku moved away and sat on a sofa.

There were two adjacent rooms. Each room could be entered through the other. The rooms could also be separated by bolting the door. Spanning the room was a large cot, the white bed linen sparkling bright. A table with chairs, a flower vase with a few stems of flowers, and a couple of easy-chairs. Ghentu set the bag carefully to one side and stood beside the window. Mamata stood at the other window, facing the sea. Her hair blew in the breeze.

The cot lay in the middle, its linen sparkling white. Butku's eyes were on Mamata. Her sari was now dishevelled. Everything was clearly visible. Butku didn't exactly gape, more like licked it all up with his eyes. He came close to Mamata and, affecting a dancer-like pose, asked, 'What are you looking at, honey?' And with that, he kissed her on the cheek. Butku then began to paw her body. Seeing this,

Ghentu slowly stood up. He came close and, like a hunter, grabbed Mamata away from Butku. He held her tight and pressed his lips on hers. His left hand frenziedly groped her bare midriff, his right hand squeezed her ample breasts. When he released her after about a minute, Mamata's face had turned red. Lipstick was smudged all over it. A tooth mark was clearly visible on one corner of her lip. Looking at herself in the mirror, somewhat angrily, somewhat satisfied and somewhat indulgently, Mamata spat out two syllables: '*De-vil!*'

Ghentu and Butku stood in front of the mirror, observing Mamata examining her face. There was a knock at the door, startling the three of them. Mamata adjusted the anchol of her sari and moved away. Butku looked at Ghentu's eyes, then, unlatching the door very cautiously, he silently stepped to one side of it. It was a hotel attendant – he had come to enquire about the dinner order. Ghentu came forward. He asked for rotis, chicken curry and various other things, after which he left. Butku shut the door and sat down. Everyone was silent now. The roar of the sea floated in from the darkness outside.

After a while, Mamata said she wanted to go to the bathroom. Ghentu got up and opened the bag carefully. He slowly took out a sari, a blouse, a bra, and so on. Mamata looked at the bra dangling from his hand. It was new, radiant white. She burst out laughing. 'Do you know the size!' For the first time, Ghentu smiled a little. 'If after so much sleeping around…' Mamata laughed, took her things and, swaying her hips, sauntered to the bathroom.

After the bathroom door was shut, Ghentu came up to Butku and whispered, 'Beware! Nothing whatsoever should arouse suspicion. I've given false names to the hotel. After finishing our business, just at the break of dawn, we must leave on the pretext of going out to see the sea. Be very careful.' Glancing at the bathroom door, he bent down and reached inside the bag. After he had finished rummaging, he said, 'It's all there, at the bottom…' He zipped up the bag, stood up straight and turned away, as if he was standing and gazing at the sea through the window.

There was silence in the room now. Butku lit a cigarette. He blew smoke rings over his nose. The sound of water running in the bathroom was drowned out by the continuous noise of the sea. After a while, Mamata came out. There were droplets of water on her neck and brow. She was clad only in the bra, she hadn't worn the blouse. The sari was loosely wound. Seeing Butku staring at her, she made a face at him. Butku ran to catch her, but Mamata moved away nimbly, saying loudly, 'Hey!' Butku didn't go any closer. He restrained himself, consoling himself with the thought that after Mamata went off to the other room, she would take off her sari and all…

There was another knock at the door. Mamata was in the other room, the door in between was half shut. Ghentu opened the door to look. It was the attendant. He came in, arranged the food on the table and left. After he left, Ghentu shut the door and fastened the bolt carefully. He pulled at the door to check whether there was any chance of it opening suddenly. Satisfied, he went and opened the bag and took out two bottles, a bottle opener and a packet of cashew nuts. Ghentu stuffed a piece of meat into his mouth and swigged directly from the bottle. As he watched Ghentu, Butku realized he was hungry too. Without further delay, he pulled out a chair and sat down at the table.

There was no sound in the room other than those of eating and drink being poured into glasses. Butku had shut the seaside window saying that he did not care about the sea. Mamata had only feebly protested as she chewed the meat. She hadn't said much, so as to not interrupt her eating. Seeing the food on the table, she had immediately pulled out a chair and sat down. Gravy dripped from her mouth. Mamata ate as if she was crazed with hunger. She chortled, 'Oh I'm eating meat after so long…' Mamata now expertly sucked the marrow out of a bone. Butku heard the sound she made – *sooan-ooo-sorhat*. It seemed that Mamata didn't care for anything right now other than the plate of meat. 'The meat's nice, really nice!' she exclaimed as she licked her lips. Butku took a gulp from the bottle and, when Mamata looked at him, he filled a glass for her. Mamata chewed on the meat with her eyes shut, downed the glass and then looked at Butku with a grin on her face.

Ghentu did not like to talk much. He was busy eating single-mindedly. He chewed the tender, soft bones, making a crunching sound. He lifted the bottle and took two more gulps. As Ghentu ate, he looked at Mamata out of the corner of his eye. Butku too looked as he ate. It was Mamata alone who did not waste time looking or doing anything else. Perhaps she had hardly eaten anything the whole day. When her plate of meat was empty, she herself poured some more booze into her glass and drank. After that, she stared greedily at Butku's plate. Butku saw Mamata staring. He saw her smile. Without so much as waiting for his approval, she snatched a chicken leg from his plate and stuffed it into her mouth. At that moment, Butku saw the inside of her mouth, her tongue, teeth, gum, yellow stains on the teeth and behind them. Mamata looked into his eyes and laughed. Butku poured booze into his glass and – *glug, glug* – gulped all of it down. Mamata's eyes sparkled now, her face had begun to acquire colour.

Ghentu's plate was empty. He was now busy uncorking the other bottle. He opened it, put the bottle to his lips and drank a little. Then he laid it down on the table. Butku had almost finished eating. Bits of chewed bones were scattered all over the table. Mamata continued to stare at him as he finished his food. There was still some meat and gravy on his plate. Her eyes were on that, but now she wasn't quite up to grabbing it. Seeing Mamata like this, gaping and hunger-crazed, a plan came into Butku's mind. He picked up a big piece of meat, held it between his teeth and signalled to Mamata. She saw through his ruse, laughed and tried to take the piece with her hand. But Butku turned his head away. Meaning, not with your hand, you must take it with your mouth. With a broad grin on her face, she bent down and tried to pull away the piece of meat. But Butku was ready. He swung around his left hand and landed a hard whack on her bare waist. The piece of meat flew out of Mamata's mouth and landed far away, on the floor. Mamata crashed down on the table, with its spread of gravy, meat, plates and rotis. Butku burst out laughing – *ha ha!* Mamata's face, smudged with meat and gravy, was red with rage.

Ghentu observed all this detachedly as he ate. Butku stopped laughing. He said, 'Why do you get angry, my sweetheart, can't you take a joke?' He wiped her face with the anchol of her sari. He then went and picked up the fallen piece of meat from the floor and shoved it into her mouth. Mamata feigned spitting it out in disgust, but didn't after all, and began eating it. She hadn't eaten her fill like this in a long time.

Ghentu watched Mamata closely. He tore open the packet of cashew nuts and threw a handful into his mouth. As soon as she saw this, Mamata did the same. She took a handful and chewed the meat and the cashews together. Her full mouth and her bobbing Adam's apple moved together, as if to the same tune. The packet of nuts emptied quickly. She swallowed hurriedly and held out her hand for another handful. Ghentu crept slowly towards her, held her by her shoulders and pulled her to his chest. Mamata had then just put another handful of nuts into her mouth and chewed away for dear life. Ghentu didn't wait, he couldn't hold on any longer. He grasped her shoulders and pressed his mouth on hers, making an *o-o-o-o-n* sound. A mix of chewed nuts and saliva entered his mouth, which he swallowed. By then, Mamata had taken control of herself. She poured herself a glassful with her left hand and gulped it all down. Saying, 'I'll teach you a lesson,' she pounced on Ghentu's chest and planted her lips on his.

Mamata was somewhat intoxicated. The anchol of her sari trailed all over the food on the table. Ghentu gently held her down on the table, the plates, meat and gravy beneath her, the chewed bones poking her. She was smeared with meat and gravy. After playing at eating her up for a while, Ghentu released her meat-and-gravy-smudged body and stepped aside, signalling towards Butku.

Butku had been watching all this and readying himself inwardly. Little by little, desire rose in him, becoming inexorable. He waited a little longer. He observed Mamata with detachment. He took another couple of swigs from the bottle. Mamata had now risen from the table and was getting a hold of herself. She was smeared with meat and gravy. Her anchol dripped with gravy. Ghentu had sat down in the chair on her right. He had stopped now, so it was Butku's turn. After that Ghentu's, turn would come again.

*The girl's lying there, have your fill!*
*Then finish the work and leave!*

A zero-watt lamp burned in the room. The windows were shut. No nonsense from outside, like the sound of the sea, entered the room. Butku took another swig from the bottle. Then he stood up. Perhaps he was a bit unsteady on his feet. Let his legs be unsteady, he wasn't drunk. He advanced towards Mamata. 'Come, my darling!' Standing at a distance, Mamata watched Butku as he came towards her. She laughed and said, 'Drunk on so little?' Butku tottered to catch Mamata. 'Beware, girl!' Mamata stepped to one side and clapped. 'Oh you brave boy! Hey, let's see you catch me!' Mamata was also unsteady on her feet. She moved aside slowly. Butku wasn't being able to catch her. Mamata suddenly turned and opened the shut window. The cold sea breeze and the roar of the waves whooshed into the room. Twisting her neck, Mamata declared, 'I'm going to watch the sea now.' 'Beware, bitch! Shut the window!' As Butku tried to approach her, Mamata moved aside. Just as he turned around after shutting the window, Mamata dashed to it and opened it again. 'Why the hell shouldn't I open the window? We've come to the sea – so won't we look at the sea?' Gnashing his teeth, Butku rushed forward, enraged. 'To hell with your sea!' He shut the window loudly and saw that Mamata's lips had become swollen with injured pride. Wondering just how long this pride would last, he again moved to catch her.

This time, Mamata did not try to escape. She stood defiantly. She saw Butku rushing towards her like a monster. For a moment, all kinds of notions in her head, she tried to run, but Butku caught hold of her anchol and the sari began coming off. Mamata looked once at Butku's face and then, for some reason, she didn't try to escape. Butku ran and grabbed her. He shoved his mouth onto hers and stroked her breast. Ghentu stood up, tottered forward and put his hands on her midriff. The buttons of the blouse popped open in his hands as Mamata resisted. He pulled off the hooks of her brassiere and exposed her fulsome pair.

Butku couldn't hold on to her properly, she kept slipping away. He clasped her body to his for a while. He nibbled her soft flesh with his teeth. After that, when his hands slipped off her again, Ghentu grabbed her. He too wasn't able to keep his two hands on the trembling body as it slipped out of his grasp. Angrily, Ghentu bit her. His teeth pierced and sank easily through the soft flesh, almost to the bone. Mamata moaned in pain, but as long as their desire remained unsatisfied, neither of them was going to stop.

Mamata's face had turned a flaming red, teeth marks on her breasts, her shoulders, her lips, her ears. Blood oozed from the cuts on her breasts. They were swollen.

Butku was still aroused. He dragged her by one arm, carried her to the bed, lifted her and laid her down with her legs spread. Mamata was still in her senses. She watched Butku hurriedly take off and fling away his shirt and trousers and advance towards her. She readied herself. Now upright, now flat, with his hands, teeth, nails and every part of his body, Butku ravaged her body. Strangely, even in her unbearable torment as she was being crushed, she wrapped her arms around Butku's hirsute back and hugged him. As she sweated and gasped for air, she pleaded in a feeble voice, 'Do open the window. Let some sea breeze in…' Butku was very busy. The feeble plea didn't reach his ears. Not paying heed to anything, he went about his business intently.

Ghentu stood, observing the proceedings. Butku sat straddling the girl, hard at work. When he finished, it would be Ghentu's turn. In a rush of blood, Ghentu decided he wasn't going to wait so long. He emptied the bottle and went over to Mamata's head and pressed his mouth down on hers. He stretched out his hands over her breasts. His nails frenziedly scratched her breasts, shoulders and neck. Every now and then Mamata struggled for breath. She wanted to open the window to get some air, but she had no way of doing that. On both sides of her were two men, grabbing, biting and squeezing her. After Butku finished, he collapsed, limp. Ghentu impatiently pushed him aside and straddled the corpse-like body lying there. His hands, legs, mouth and nails moved simultaneously. Mamata still tried weakly to flail her arms and legs. But her body began to grow limp under Ghentu's crushing grip.

After a while, Ghentu noticed that Mamata was strangely still. No sign of life in her body, as if it was a lump of wet dough. 'Hey, has the doll copped it!' He put his ear on her breast and listened. The heart was beating all right, she wasn't dead. Maybe she had just fainted in fear or something. If she died, why, all the fun would be spoilt! No joy unless she was alive! So Ghentu poured the remaining drops from the bottle into Mamata's mouth. Worried, he spread out the sari in his hands and fluttered it. After a while, he got up and opened the window to let some air in. The wind and the roar of the sea entered the room. Butku noticed this, but he didn't say anything under the circumstances. Instead, he brought some water and splashed it on Mamata's shoulders and neck.

Mamata returned to her senses in a few minutes. She was able to sit up. Seeing her sit up, Ghentu's and Butku's faces lit up with smiles. The pair advanced and kissed her cheeks a few times. They pawed and squeezed her all over for a while. The breeze blew in through the window, a gusty sea breeze. Mamata gazed blankly in that direction. After they had more or less enjoyed her in her sitting position, they rose and glanced briefly at Mamata's face. Then Butku rose and shut the window. Ghentu went and rummaged in the bag. He took out a long knife. He pressed the spring mechanism and, in a flash, the blade of the knife sprang out. Mamata's face instantly turned purple. She tried to stand up. She stood up and then stepped backwards. Perhaps she let out a moan, but the cry didn't carry beyond the closed doors and windows. Mamata stepped backwards. Ghentu stepped forward. Time ticked. Butku stood watching. Ghentu advanced, Mamata retreated. At one point, she tried to say something, but it wasn't clear whether her lips moved or not. Retreating, Mamata had reached the wall, she couldn't retreat any further.

Ghentu advanced with very slow steps. The blade of the knife was raised, light flashed on it. Mamata then closed her eyes and put out her hands as if to avert something. 'No-oh-oh…' Butku rushed towards Ghentu. 'What's the hurry! Let's play with her for a while.' He thought of a new game. He pushed Ghentu aside and snatched the knife. Swishing it this way and that, he held it near her breast, but didn't stab her. Laughing out of the corner of his mouth, he said, 'You're so scared of dying! All right then. I won't kill you… But you'll have to do whatever I ask you to.' Mamata was still, flattened against the wall, her eyes shut. Butku prodded her stomach with the blunt edge of the blade. 'Hey you! Look! And keep looking!' Saying so, Butku and Ghentu swayed their bodies, looked at each other and laughed. *Ho ho! Ha ha! Hee hee!*

Mamata trembled with fear and raised her hands to try to fend them off. She tried to say something, but no sound escaped her lips. *Ho ho!* They laughed, looking at each other's exposed organs, while she cringed against the wall at the sound of their laughter. 'Mamata, why are you so scared of dying, dear? Everybody has to go to the Nimtala burning ghat one day!' They kept laughing, as if they were playing throw-and-catch with their words. The bared steel flashed.

Mamata's eyes were shut. Trembling, terrified, she wanted to say something. 'Speak love, speak! Say what's your final wish! *Ha ha!*' Butku laughed. Mamata trembled violently. Her back was to the wall. In front of her was the shining steel blade. 'I'll give you one last chance to save yourself,' said Butku, smirking. 'This knife – I'll throw this knife of mine on the bed. Whoever grabs it first shall live. See if you can try and live!'

Ghentu didn't laugh now. He was taken aback by the state Butku's was in. Butku continued to laugh crazily and asked, 'Got that? The knife will be thrown away. You can go and get it first. Try!' He moved towards the corner of the room, near Mamata. As Mamata heard these words, she suddenly sprang to life. Her eyes gleamed. There were beads of perspiration on her brow and nose. Butku played with the knife, tossed it from one hand to the other a couple of times, laughed. Then he flung it. As it landed on the bed, Mamata raced like an arrow and grabbed the base of the knife. In a flash, Ghentu and Butku leapt to two sides. There was astonishment on their eyes and faces. Now Mamata brandished the knife. She couldn't decide in which direction to advance, which was the way to survival. She stood and panted, her eyes on the pair. Balls of fire flashed in those eyes. A few silent moments. Nobody moved. Suddenly, signalling Butku with his eyes, Ghentu sped towards her. He grabbed Mamata's hand, the one which clutched the knife. Butku ran and held the other hand firmly, saying, 'Come, my love!' They began to grope and paw Mamata's spent body crazily.

Mamata struggled, but with other mouths and lips pressed to her mouth, her voice was inaudible. After they played with her body like this for some time, her condition became worse. Drops of blood welled up between her legs. A thin stream of blood ran down her thighs to her knees. Seeing the blood, Ghentu made a sign to Butku. With his hands, Butku held Mamata's arms and mouth. Ghentu raised the knife, looked at her awhile, then stabbed her deep in the chest, plunging the knife downwards. The torso trembled. Butku was unable to hold her still with his two hands. The nineteen-year-old body shuddered in a valiant attempt to survive. Crimson blood flowed down to the floor. The yellowish innards hung out, the two legs trembled agitatedly. After holding her firmly for a few minutes, Butku released his grasp. The body fell flat on the floor.

Butku's hands were bloody too. As he wiped his hands on the sari, he looked at the gaping innards, at the fleshy region at the base of the abdomen and the two legs which trembled before gradually becoming still. A thick stream of blood flowed down the side of the stomach and accumulated on the floor. Butku wiped his hands and threw the sari at Ghentu who stood watching Mamata die. He then cleaned the knife thoroughly and wiped his hands. 'Any more cigarettes?' asked Butku. Wiping away the blood from the base of the knife, Ghentu said, 'There's a pack in the bag, take it out.'

*1968*

# Amber Light at Park Street Crossing

The beggar was dying as he lay under the cold, relentless, flashing light. On one side was the lurking darkness of the Maidan; on the other, gaudy Chowringhee; and in between, beneath a traffic light post, lay the beggar. His staff, tin pan, loincloth, the hair on his face, the froth on his mouth, the odour of excreta dried up on the soles of his two feet, all these – for that matter, his shrivelled, crooked, broken body – if only everything were wiped out, sanctified rain would shower on this place. Three girls wearing beautiful, flowing saris and snapping peanuts with their teeth would search for a green spot on the Maidan. They would say: 'I re-al-ly love to get wet in this rain!'

In the darkness, a group of people tried to move in procession in one direction. The Studebaker braked and stopped in front of the red light on Park Street. The sound of giggling floated out from the car and the beggar's life-breath became laboured. The colours red-blue-yellow formed and dissolved in front of his eyes. Standing in the middle of the

Khidirpur Bridge in the night turned desolate and silent, a lunatic thumped his chest loudly and shouted, 'We'll kill and seize Jhumjhuma – from today!' He screamed, 'Hear, everybody hear, the beggar is dying!' But his voice was drowned out by the voice of All India Radio: 'When our national flag was fixed atop the podium where the prime minister delivered his speech, a crow – a vile, shrewd, devil of a crow – shat on the flag and flew off. We are hunting for that crow and, when we find it, we shall spear it, hang it, wring its neck; we shall thus mete out fitting punishment for shitting on our national flag.'

The blood in the bosom of some grew red; of some, black; and of some, white. When all of the last few drops of the beggar's lifeblood turned white, the beggar prostrated himself, paid obeisance and prayed to the earth for death. Somewhere, someone had kept a grave ready in advance. Everyone knew people would die, just as even dogs and jackals die on the streets. Nevertheless, on the Khidirpur Bridge, in the desolation, the solitary lunatic screamed and tried to convince somebody: 'Hear, the beggar is dying, the beggar is really dying!'

At that moment, two callow youths entered a bar on Chowringhee. Another kissed his companion under a tree in the Maidan. The paan-seller at the kerb sold a zarda paan. The traffic light at Park Street turned amber. The boy vending flowers sold a string of bel garlands to a lady inside a halted car. And under the Monument, a middle-aged magician performed a money-doubling act and drew applause from the assembled crowds. A struggling people's procession passed the spot, shouting a slogan like 'Everything must be expropriated!' Some looked at the beggar dying, but they didn't have the time – got to go to the public meeting at the Maidan! They went off with their festoons. Their slogans, like the deep sigh of the boy standing in front of the restaurant, who had not eaten all day, were squandered away on Chowringhee's gleaming black thoroughfare.

Repeated announcements over the radio, a fire-spewing speech – the subject being the crow's shitting on the national flag. Police detectives have been sent all over, that wicked crow must be found, must be apprehended. From somewhere, a flower fragrance wafted. From somewhere, the smell of blood wafted. Someone, somewhere, sang a stanza of Rabindrasangeet. Somewhere, somebody searched for the skull of an unclaimed corpse. On the Khidirpur Bridge, the lunatic beat his chest and sang: 'We'll fight and seize Jhumjhuma!' The tide splashed in on the Ganga. At the bar, the youth noisily broke a glass and affected a heroic laugh. A Frenchman, brown beard, pale eyes, roamed the streets of Calcutta, hauling a camera. Seeing the beggar dying, he said, 'Ten rupees bakshish, hold on for two more minutes,' and pounced. 'I'll take your picture, it'll be a marvellous art film.' The lunatic, the same one from Khidirpur, said, 'Sir, the beggar is dying!' He said, 'I piss on the face of your art!' He said, 'We'll kill and seize Jhumjhuma!' and beat his chest.

A cold breeze blew. The traffic light went from red to amber to green. Someone spoke. Someone cried. Someone quarrelled. Someone counted money. Someone made love. Someone painted a picture. Someone weighed something. Someone was born. Someone died. Someone looked into darkness. Someone saw the light.

The beggar had earlier been human. He liked to crunch-munch chicken legs. He liked to see beautiful women in the cinema. He liked to eat phuchkas at the Maidan. He liked to smoke cigarettes. He liked to sleep with a young woman in his arms. After his pauperization was complete, when the hair on his face turned grey, his shoulders stooped and he learnt to swallow the hunger of his stomach, he had no desires. Two scholars argued:

'The beggar wanted to live.'

'Who doesn't want to live?'

A group of people at the Red Road intersection tried all night long to find their way. Someone coughed and coughed and then couldn't stop himself from vomiting red blood in front of Mahatma Gandhi at Park Street. The girl who stood waiting for prey revealed her dry red throat as she yawned. Some people listened eagerly to the night's last news bulletin on the radio. 'There's no clue of the crow that shat on the national flag and made off.' Dejected, they went off to go to bed and fall asleep, clasping their wives and dreaming happy dreams. And the battling, tattered beggar was dying, the whiplash of the flashing light on his chest. He saw the money-doubling act. He heard on the radio: 'Our country shall become golden, no one shall die for want of food!'; he heard: 'We will not tolerate the insult to the national flag, we will not tolerate it!'; he heard the national song, 'Rich with thy streams, thy orchards… verdant fields'; heard 'This fight is for life, this fight must be won!'; heard Rabindrasangeet: 'O helmsman, set afloat the boat on the river of peace ahead'. A dog ferreting for food dug its snout into a dustbin. A youth seized pleasure by squeezing a woman's breast. The magician showed his money-doubling act...

Driven to despair, the lunatic standing on the Khidirpur Bridge then cried out, his face turned to the Maidan, 'A beggar is dying!' But no one heard him. Those who made love in the darkness went on doing so. He then came to the junction of the Ganga's well-lit promenade and cried out, 'A beggar is dying!' No one heard him. People went on eating their moshla-muri or peanuts or ice cream. He went to the Chowringhee junction and cried out, his arms raised high, 'Hear, people, hear! A beggar is dying!' Nobody heard. A man brought his face close and whispered, 'Brother, do you know where booze is available?' A group of people crowded around a radio listening to the news. The lunatic went up to them and said meekly, 'A beggar is dying.' Without paying any heed to his words, they discussed how that scheming crow could be found, why it had not been found yet, the dishonour to our national flag. In a final bid, the lunatic then crept rapidly up to the top of the Monument. He took off his waist-cloth, cut his finger and drew with blood a symbol on it, and waved it animatedly in the air. He screamed, 'Hear, people, hear! A beggar is dying!' But his voice did not reach the ground. Down below, the magician went on with his money-doubling act to tumultuous applause. The lunatic screamed out again, with all the strength in his lungs, enough to make the Monument quake. But the people below were engrossed in the money-doubling act. No voice reached their ears. Exasperated beyond measure, he came down and said, 'May the beggar die, become an evil spirit and possess you! May he break your neck!' He said, 'We'll fight and seize

Jhumjhuma!' Thumping his chest, he walked away towards the darkness of Khidirpur. And the flag splattered with his blood fluttered over the Monument all night.

*1969*

# The Dagger

Someone called out from behind: 'Hooeey Sudas! Where're you goin', pal?' He didn't look back. The dead body still hung from the tree branch, feet bound, head downwards. Blood poured steadily from the nose and had dripped down and wet the place. He saw the wizened old bird sitting in its cage. It tested the iron mesh with its beak. Every once in a while, it fluttered its wings and screeched: 'Sudas! Hooeey Sudas! Where're you goin', pal?'

He had stolen the dagger from his friend's house. It belonged to an earlier age. Sheathed in a purple muslin case, the dagger's hilt was of ivory, shaped like a horse's head. Every now and then, making sure no one was around, he felt its sharp edge. Jackals howled from the clearings between the trees and shrubs in the dark night. He heard his mother say, 'Why do you look so worried, Sudas?' Startled, he replied, 'Where? Not at all!' He ran, with the dagger concealed in his pocket. He ran through fields, banks, woods and forests, until he finally reached Kasim Miya's stable. He stood panting. The cage swayed with the bird's fluttering. It cried out: 'Sudas! Hooeey Sudas! Where're you goin', pal?'

Kasim Miya's stable was deserted. The horse carriage trade did not quite exist any more. Stroking his grey-streaked beard, he said, 'The city now wants motor cars, we're done for, and with us this trade will come to an end… Do you know, young master, what a grand thing this double carriage used to be! It was a matter of honour for the babus. Fluttering the pleats of their dhotis, fragrant with attar, the babus and bibis used to go out for a spin… And now…' Kasim Miya lamented and absent-mindedly stroked his beard. Strewn all around him were parts, relics and broken wheels of forsaken carriages. In one corner, like a lone symbol, a horse, blinkers over its eyes, chewed grass from the feeding bag hung on its neck. Every now and then, it stamped its hooves on the wooden floor, every once in a while, it neighed – *Aayn-han-han-han!* – as if to register its protest against something.

Blood dripped from the body hanging on the tree and wet the place. As kids, some people used to kill tomcats like this. They'd tie a rope round its neck and hang it from a banana tree. It would cry and mewl all night as it tried to free itself. The cat would be dead the next morning. A group of them would go in the morning to see the dead cat. By mid-morning, thousands of big black ants would have trooped in and devoured its eyes. At night, fireflies could be seen glowing around the dead body.

Sudas panted. Kasim Miya was saying something. 'What's happened to you, little master, why are you panting like this?' Pressing his hand over his pocket, he replied, 'No, nothing's happened.' He said, 'Do you know, Kasim chacha, a wild animal has possessed me, and it's restless. Right here' – he pointed to the centre of his chest. He continued, 'Beyond the road, on the creek-side, I saw a dark-skinned, lanky man roaming around, creeping on all fours. He was going around sniffing the dirty places at the creek-side.' Kasim Miya replied, 'What's new about that, little master, the people on the other side have declared war. They say, we want to work and survive, we want to live with dignity.'

The stable-bound horse, ribs protruding, eyes blinkered, stamped its hooves on the wooden floor. Every once in a while it neighed – *Aayn-han-han-han!* An eerie sound, as if it was protesting against something. The sound startled Sudas. He gripped the dagger concealed in his pocket.

Sudas had no desire to steal the dagger. But as he stood amidst the old knives, daggers and swords laid out inside the room, somehow, something happened to him. His heart beating fast, he was about to run from there when he saw a huge buffalo head with the horns sticking out, and to his right, a complete tiger-skin with the face frozen in a snarl. Kasim Miya was an old man. He puffed at a bidi. Outside, the darkness thickened and, in that darkness, Kasim gazed on vacantly.

He felt very uneasy in the semi-darkness. Absent-mindedly, haphazardly, he cleared woods and forests. He saw humans and dogs ferreting for food in the same garbage bin. The bird called out. It fluttered its wings and screeched, 'What'll you do with this dagger, Sudas? Return it! Return it!' He didn't know what he would do with it. He kept going, leaving behind all the people, settlements and trees.

The weapon was held firmly in his pocket. Every once in a while, he took it out and examined it. He gazed at its purple muslin case, embroidered in red and green. He drew it out by its ivory hilt.

With the horse's eerie neigh – *Aayn-han-han-han!* – the silence of night was shattered. The dagger almost fell out of his hand. He said, 'What will I do with this? I didn't want things to turn out this way.' He looked in all directions to see if anyone had caught him unawares, and then he hurriedly concealed it in his pocket.

Two youths with serious faces emerged from somewhere and said, 'What'll you do with that, Sudas? Give it to us.' He held it firmly in his grip. Grave-faced, they returned to the dark lakeside in the same way they had emerged from the darkness. Only the fireflies glowed dimly. Jackals howled from somewhere far away. Blood dripped steadily from the nose of that dead body hanging upside down from the tree. Big black ants gathered there.

The long country road snaked past the creek in the dim moonlight. Every now and then, the muffled sound of someone crying floated by. And sometimes, the sound of someone laughing. As he went along the red-brick road in the twilit darkness, passing cyclists cried out, 'Where are you headed, Sudas, in this darkness? Towards the desolate ruins of the fortress?' Startled, Sudas said, 'Nowhere. Nowhere at all.'

Kasim Miya stroked his beard. His emaciated horse, blinkered, chewed away at the grass from its feeding bag. He said gravely, 'The times are frightful, little master… be careful where you go. Don't go near the lake after dark.'

'Why, what's happened there?' 'Oh nothing at all.' Kasim Miya seemed to be withholding something, as if he wasn't bold enough to say it. He saw his bird fluttering its wings in the cage. It didn't eat the grains given to it. He saw the old beggar woman sitting at the station with her hands laid out in the hope of alms. He saw the cunning jackal with the stolen hen swiftly slipping away from the light of the homestead into the brown darkness.

As his throat was parched, he went towards the lake's ghat for a drink of water. The moon rose in the east over the Radha-Govind temple. He saw the reflection of the moon in the lake. Gazing at it, he wondered whether he should throw the dagger away into the water... That would bring matters to a close, he wouldn't be troubled any more. But he didn't throw it away. He held on to it as if for dear life. That ancient, engraved dagger's blade gleamed in the moonlight. He said, 'I can't just throw it away now!' But soon enough, he began to wonder what he would do with it.

At Romen Deb's house, many daggers like this hung on the walls of the drawing room, including several larger than this one. There were so many kinds of guns and pistols too. Romen's father, twirling his moustache explained, 'All these are so old, have been used in war. History, full of history!'

Standing beside the lake and looking at the moonlit water, he wondered why he took it. Why? Crickets chirped. The entire lakeside was redolent with the fragrance of mango and bel. The steps going down to the water were old and run-down. Tramping over dry leaves, he emerged from the lakeside.

From its cage, his pet bird kept calling: 'Hooeey Sudas! Where're you goin', pal? Hooeey Sudas!' Mother asked, 'Why are you so late, Sudas?' 'Just like that. I was sitting at the lakeside. Do you know, Ma, nowadays some people come there, a band of them, to hear the blue-throated cuckoo's cry. They have dry blood on their hands, red and blue feathers on their head.' 'You're full of trouble! Don't be going there!' 'Why, Ma?' After a pause, peering into his eyes, she said, 'You appear a little strange today, Sudas.' He replied, 'That's not surprising, Ma, for I saw humans and dogs ferreting for food from the same garbage bin.' He then showed his mother the place wet with blood, where blood had been dripping endlessly through the nose of the dead body.

The horse neighed in Kasim Miya's stable – *Aayn-han-han-han!* Kasim just sat in the darkness, swatting mosquitoes, puffing on a bidi once in a while. He said, 'All those days are gone, young master. Won't come back! Used to gallop – *clip-clop! clip-clop!* – with babu and bibi along the road to the old fort. The people walking on the road would step aside. Babu's double-carriage! Stand aside! Stand aside! I'll be gone, and with me everything will be over.'

Sudas just couldn't sleep at night. He heard someone whispering at the window, 'What will you do with that, Sudas? Give it, give it to us!' He had hidden it, buried it under the mango tree at the lakeside. He thought – now I'm at peace, no one will find it! In the middle of the night, he saw a few jackals digging up the place in search of the dead body. He ran out and, screaming, hurled stones to chase away the jackals. Their eyes like burning coals, the jackals hovered nearby. They didn't go away.

Sudas's heart thumped. 'I shouldn't have taken it.' His sleepless eyes scanned the sky and he ran his hand through his dishevelled hair as he roamed the lakeside all night, like a madman. He kept seeing the humans and dogs together, squabbling and eating bones and remains from the same garbage bin. He heard his mother's voice from far away: 'Don't go there, Sudas, don't go, Suuuudaaaas!' His caged pet bird screeched: 'Hooeey Sudas!'

Ill at ease, Sudas said, 'Do you know, Kasim chacha, I've stolen a dagger. And do you know, I don't know what I'll do with it!' Then, absent-mindedly running his fingers through his hair, he said, 'I didn't really want to steal it, you know. Don't know what happened all of a sudden ... Do you know, in Romen Deb's house, there are fabulous daggers, swords, guns, tiger skins, buffalo horns, just like in a museum...' He felt an ache inside his chest. He turned blue in the face in agony. His muttered words were muffled by the sound of the horse's neighing – *Aayn-han-han-han!* – coming from Kasim Miya's stable. Just that one skinny horse in Kasim Miya's stable. It silently champed on the grass from the feeding bag. Every now and then, it swished its tail, every once in a while, it stamped its hooves – *thok! thok!* – on the wooden floor, every now and then, it neighed – *Aayn-han-han-han!* – as if it wished to say something. Kasim Miya said, 'It's time, I'll go, my horse will go too.' He threw away the bidi, rose and stroked the ribs protruding on the horse's flank. He said, 'Be very careful, little master, terrible times now. Don't stray from the road and go to the lakeside!'

When the ache in his chest became more acute, Sudas stepped onto the road and walked distractedly. A cool breeze blew in the darkness of the night, bringing with it the gentle fragrance of mango and bel. Their eyes glowing like torches, a few jackals hovered around him. They had soaked in the blood dripping from that dead body and returned blood-crazed. He felt awful. Occasionally, he felt pleased. Every once in a while, he thought he hadn't wanted all this to happen. Every now and then, he remembered those people who had come to hear the cuckoo's cry. Stale blood staining their hands, they had come to hear a beautiful birdsong.

The whole place was desolate. The moonlight lit up the ruins of the crumbling ancient fort and the undulating, once-regal, red-earth road. He was not afraid. He walked along, the dagger concealed in his pocket.

Agitated, absent-minded, he trudged on. Every once in a while, he heard the faint cry of his mother: 'O Sudas!' He then tried to bring to mind the sight of humans and dogs fighting over food beside the same garbage bin. Every now and then, his pet bird fluttered its wings inside the cage. 'Hooeey Sudas! Where're you goin', pal? Hooeey Sudas!' He wondered where he would go to ease the pain inside him. Where could he go? Every once in a while, he remembered Romen's father's words: 'Do you know, Sudas, all these knives and daggers, guns and pistols that you see displayed on the wall here have made history at one time. History, full of history!'

In Kasim Miya's stable, that solitary emaciated horse, eyes blinkered, occasionally stamped its hooves on the wooden floor and occasionally swished its tail to drive away flies. But nowadays, it neighed frequently – *Aayn-han-han-han!* – as if to protest against something. Puffing on his bidi, Kasim Miya said, 'Along with you all, our times are also coming to an end, little master! Be very careful! Don't be going to the lakeside after dark!'

After walking for a long time, Sudas eventually began to tire. He saw himself walking endlessly, caged by the moonlight. Ahead of him lay the ruins of the old fort. He advanced mechanically in that direction. Then he remembered the corpse. He felt a constant unbearable ache inside his chest. He decided he would get rid of the troublesome weapon in this desolate moonlight, in the ghostly precincts of this old fort, and leave. 'After I leave, I shall join that band of people – those with dry blood staining their hands, who had come to hear the cuckoo's call…'

Tired, he sat down in the majestic ruins of the ancient fort. He recalled Romen's father saying: 'History, full of history!' He recalled Kasim Miya's lament: 'It'll all end with me, I'll be dead, and this old horse of mine will be dead too!' Tears streamed down from the blinkered eyes of the horse. Kasim stroked its bony side and comforted it.

All the tears and blood came together and became one. Clouds shrouded the moon briefly. Darkness enveloped the stone walls of that ancient fort. Tearing his hair out with his two hands, Sudas screamed like a madman: 'I didn't want this! I didn't want this!' Feebly, he took out the dagger. As he was about to hurl it into the darkness of the fort, he saw countless hands on the stone walls of that ancient fort. Countless agitated hands had left their palm prints in syllables of blood.

*1971*

# Fairy Girl

As Sukhamoy entered his room after bathing in the sea, he saw Rani was dead. He had never imagined Rani dying like this. He was shocked. He went and called Rajat, Tamal and Dipen.

Rajat, Tamal and Dipen too were shocked to find Rani dead. It was the middle of the night. The light of a candle fluttered frailly in the room. Gazing at it, Sukhamoy realized he was scared. He looked at the other faces one by one. In the dim light of the candle, the shadow of fear seemed to hover over each face.

Sukhamoy wondered what they ought to do now. They had come with Rani to this small seaside town in the hope of a few days of pleasure. An incident like this should never have taken place. There was no need for Rani to die. Sukhamoy began to feel terribly angry with Rani. Just one thought came to their mind: they were simply not prepared for something like this. Together they began to think about what they ought to do now.

Rani's dead body lay in the room, covered by a white sheet. The four of them stood helplessly on four sides. As he stood there, it struck Sukhamoy that something must be done. Come morning, the matter would become public. There would be trouble. And none of them wanted to get embroiled in any kind of difficulty.

Sukhamoy looked at everyone's faces. He wanted to ask them what they should do now. But none of them could think of anything. Rani's dead body lay in the middle of the room, covered by a white sheet. In the dim light, the shadows of the four fluttered on the walls.

Suddenly, of those four standing people, Tamal seemed to make some movement. He had been a little more passionate about Rani than the others. Sukhamoy saw that Tamal's lips were moving. To encourage Tamal, Sukhamoy asked, 'Do you want to say something, Tamal?'

Tamal lifted his face and looked at Sukhamoy. After that, his eyes scanned all the things in the room and then, like before, he became still.

Once again, Sukhamoy looked at everyone's faces, one by one. They had all turned stonily silent. Rani's dead body lay in the middle of the room, covered by a white sheet. The flickering light of the candle fluttered all over the room.

'You people, say something! You must say something!' Sukhamoy's voice seemed to agitate the other three bodies in the room. Everyone became a bit restless. But the agitation soon subsided and, finally, they were still again.

Observing the situation, Sukhamoy was astonished. Something like this ought not to have happened. But not a squeak out of them, and the night was about to end. They were bound to get into trouble once it was morning.

Sukhamoy restlessly paced the room now. Something must be done. Something had to happen. He shouted out, 'Have you all turned to stone or what? Say something, for heaven's sake!'

But no other voice, no other sound was heard in the room. Those three people remained silent as before. Between them lay Rani's corpse, covered by a white sheet, visible in the dim light the candle cast over the room. It then struck Sukhamoy that it was the lure of Rani that had brought them here. Rani had been the only attraction for them. Seeing Rani dead, they had lost all interest in this place.

Sukhamoy smiled wryly at the thought. He stared at everyone's faces. All these dead faces could be awakened right now! They would stir up like living bodies just now to claim their individual rights!

Sukhamoy went and stood beside the dead body. 'I want to say a few things.' He paused for a while. 'We were the ones who brought Rani along. We had rights over Rani when she was alive. We fed her and clothed her. We used her when we needed to. Rani was our joint property...' A soft buzz was now audible from the three people who stood there.

'We watched over Rani's health. We watched over what she wore. Because we knew that if that fairy-like body got spoilt, Rani would be of no use to us. If she stopped looking good, we wouldn't need Rani. Just as people sell off old and dry cows to the butcher, we too would have had to sell Rani off somewhere.'

Now Sukhamoy paused for a longer while. He scanned everyone's faces once. There was a glimmer of reaction in those eyes.

'But midway, everything was turned upside down. Rani betrayed us. We brought her to this seaside town so that all of us could have some fun. We would bathe her naked. We would be excited all night by the warmth of her body. But she went and died. Not once did she think about all the money that we had spent tending to her needs. Not once was she grateful to us. She didn't think it necessary to inform anyone. *Pop!* – and she just died, without anyone knowing. Shouldn't she have told us before dying that she was going to die? Now, you tell me, isn't this treachery?'

The three figures now nodded their heads. They agreed that it was treachery.

'If that is so, if it is indeed treachery, then according to the laws of the civilized world, she deserves severe punishment. But we are decent people. We have faith in democracy. We come to terms with one another to erase differences and bitterness. We can't lose faith suddenly. Because we've learnt that it is a sin to lose faith in humanity. We can't become uncivilized just because Rani betrayed us by dying suddenly without telling any of us a thing. We can't go and ask for compensation for Rani from her father. We are decent folk. We wouldn't go so far.

'But injustice must be punished. Or else, democracy cannot work, the earth couldn't go on, the sun and the moon wouldn't rise and set. Unless those who pollute this sacred earth of god with their unjust actions are punished, why, it would amount to tolerating injustice! A terrible punishment ought to be meted out for the injustice committed by Rani for dying without informing us. For the way she suddenly left us in danger.

'But we are decent men. We are civilized men. We can't be rude towards Rani just because she committed an act of injustice. Besides, her fairy-like body gave us pleasure so many times. Considering all this, I have thought of a course of action. We kept Rani. We fed and clothed her well every day. By that token, we can claim something from Rani. By virtue of this claim we want to punish her.'

Rajat, Tamal and Dipen too now screamed out in one voice: 'Yes, indeed! We're not yet willing to forfeit all our claims over Rani!'

Sukhamoy laughed and said, 'I know. I know our minds. I can swear on the whole wide civilized world and say that there's nothing sinful whatsoever in any of our minds. We know the butcher does not throw away anything from the animal sold to him. He sells the meat and the blood, of course, but the skin, horns and even the intestines are not discarded. We can very well claim a little something from dead Rani. That's well within our rights.'

The three of them exclaimed simultaneously, 'Of course we have a right!'

'We liked various parts of Rani's body when she was alive. By virtue of the aforementioned rights, we can now cut out all those parts from Rani's body. There's no sin in that. Nothing unfair about it. We are merely exercising our own rights!'

As soon as the declaration was made, the three men leapt. With a single pull, they removed the white sheet from the body. The blade of the knife in their hands flashed in the candlelight. They moved speedily and were soon busy cutting out the flesh from various special parts of the corpse. The light from the candle filled the whole room. One man expertly dug the knife in his hand into the left breast and, with a circular motion, deftly took out the whole breast in his palm. The corners of the room were in darkness. The light from the candle did not reach there. Another man cut out and held the fleshy part of the lower abdomen and was about to take his pleasure by licking it with his tongue. The third man cut out the other breast.

Without any further delay, Sukhamoy joined the band. The body was full of gaping craters. Bloody. Sukhamoy pushed and turned the body around, looking for some juicy piece. Nothing nice remained. But among the remains, like an expert butcher, he spotted a bloody thigh. The fleshy thigh was still intact. As if he were slicing off the flesh of a kid goat, he cut out the flesh from the shapely thigh. Then he tried to find excitement by fondling that soft flesh.

The candle burnt in the room, but its light did not reach everyone's eyes. They were all busy with their lumps of flesh. Their faces were extremely agitated, eyes elated, and a kind of growling sound emanated from their throats. Perspiration dripped from their exhausted bodies, yet they were rapt and busy with their hungers for a long while. The candle burnt dimly and, in its light, their shadows danced chaotically. Lost in themselves, they were aroused by those dissected parts and sections and fantasized about Rani's live body to the very last moment.

By and by, their movements subsided. Having long nursed those fantasies in their hearts, they dropped down on all fours, like dogs in heat, and panted. Gradually their excitement abated. They returned to their senses. The night was coming to an end. Some arrangement needed to be made about the dead body. Sukhamoy still lay on the bloody lumps of flesh. The heap of flesh was flattened under the weight of his chest and hips as he panted. After a while, he stood up. His hairy chest was daubed in dark blood. Everything in the room was topsy-turvy. Rani's body now looked the way an animal carcass would after its flesh had been torn out by vultures.

All this while, Sukhamoy hadn't looked at Rani's eyes. Now he felt the two eyes staring pointedly at him. Sukhamoy was a bit scared. He turned around and went to another part of the room. Then, with great trepidation, he turned around again and looked. It did look as if Rani was glaring at him. An icy fear seized his heart. His heart seemed to tremble. The room looked spooky in the candlelight. The distorted corpse lay in the middle of the room. In three corners lay the three youths, each one in his own posture. Moving gently, they lapped up their pleasure. And in the middle, the corpse seemed to stare haughtily at Sukhamoy. He felt as if his life was in danger. Opening the window and poking his head out, he gazed at the sea. Dazzling moonlight outside. The roar of the sea floated in. The vast seashore, desolate, desert-like, immense. It was close to dawn now. He felt perturbed. He called out to the other three youths.

They rose quickly, as if from slumber. There was a purple haze of intoxication in everyone's eyes. Sukhamoy shared his anxiety with them. It was very dangerous for the corpse to be lying here like this. There would be no trace left behind if they went and buried it in the seashore. Everyone would be safe.

Each of them now wrapped up their lumps of flesh in handkerchiefs and kept them in secure places. They could be used again when needed. They then arrived at a decision. It was best to take the corpse outside. If they buried it in the sand it would never be found by anyone. The four of them took the ravaged body outside. Terrifying bright moonlight outside. The roar of the sea nearby was clearly audible. The white moonlight enveloping the ghostly black sea froze each one of their hearts. They were seized by an inner dread. But none of them could say anything to anyone else. The four youths carried the corpse together to take it far away. Moonlight shone on the deep craters in the corpse. They could see how repulsive the dissected body looked. Sand everywhere, here and there a clump of thorny shrubs. A flood of moonlight, and the sea's deep roar. They felt as if they were walking through some terrifying nightmare landscape. As they walked on the soft wet sand, they made four sets of heavy footprints.

Sand blew in the wind on the seashore. Gusts of chilly breeze hit their faces and eyes. Every now and again, the moonlight, the sea and the dark earth appeared to become one in their eyes. Nonetheless, they trudged on in search of a safe refuge where Rani's body could be hidden from people's sight. But they could not find a suitable place. As they walked, their bodily strength began to wane. Their legs ached. Their chests heaved. They realized they were exhausted. They did not have any more strength to lift and carry the young girl's corpse any further. Very soon, they came to a halt. They looked at each other's faces, trying to find some answer. Finally, putting the corpse down on the sand, they sat down in a circle, gasping for breath.

As they sat on the sand, they were struck by a terrible fear. They could not help hearing their own hearts thumping. The thumping seemed to fuse with the roar of the sea. In that primitive desolation, these four living beings grew increasingly perturbed for some unknown reason. They examined each other's faces again and again. But they were unable to say anything. Nothing remained to be said. Sukhamoy was the most worried of the lot. He felt an icy chill inside him. He spotted a palm tree across a sand dune. He saw the seashore stretching to the horizon. He saw the terrifying black sea. Nothing was clearly visible. But the sound of the sea was unceasing, primeval. It seemed to rush forth and crash into his ribs. Gazing at all this, his eyes finally returned to Rani's corpse. He felt the two eyes now stare terrifyingly at him. He tried to turn his face away. But Rani's face seemed to pull at him. Helplessly, he looked at it again. Even his spine quaked in fear. Rani stared at him and smiled.

Sitting in that seaside moonlight, Sukhamoy broke into a cold sweat. What was this! Bravely trying to steel himself, he looked again at the dead face. Now he saw Rani's face melt into tears. Tears flowed out of the corners of the eyes and down her cheeks. Sukhamoy rubbed his eyes. He tried desperately to be normal. With the back of his hand, he wiped the sweat off his brow. Rani's blood was still on his hands. Cold, dark, congealed blood.

Something strange was happening to Sukhamoy now. He seemed to have lost the ability to think. A trembling sensation swept through his entire body and rose up to his head. Attempting to reach out and touch the youth sitting beside him, he saw that he too was staring fixedly at Rani's face. Sukhamoy looked at the faces of the three men in turn. The shadow of terror hung over all three faces. They were now seized by an awful terror. They did not want to sit any more in this deserted beach with the hideous corpse. Sukhamoy's body turned to ice. The deserted seashore in the vast moonlit darkness seemed to be full of only darkness and more darkness. Sukhamoy could not see or hear anything except the deep thunder of the sea exploding in a terrifying roar inside his head. He was at a complete loss now. He had lost all sensation. In front of him, he could see the three youths, terror-stricken, stand up, leave the corpse behind and run for their lives through that impossibly white moonlight.

Sukhamoy's senses deserted him. For the last time, full of fear, he tried to look at the corpse. Now a smile lit up the face. The very next moment, he saw a look of frightful horror on the same face. And the next moment, he thought the face melted into tears. All feeling abandoned Sukhamoy. He tried with all his might to remain composed. A strange kind of terror assailed him from within. He imagined that if he stayed there any longer, Rani's dead body would rise again and ask for her lost body parts to be restored. Sukhamoy tried his best to stand up. He wanted to run away from there. His hands, feet, hips – none of them seemed to function normally. Dazzling moonlight showered down haplessly from the sky above, and the steady, immaculate sound of the sea beside.

Moving like a zombie, Sukhamoy wanted to escape from there. As he ran helplessly in that desolate seashore, he felt Rani's corpse had risen with a terrifying cry. Guffawing, it chased him. It was about to catch him.

*1968*

# Blood

There was a jungle of wild orange berries around the disused path skirting the pond. It extended right till the veranda of the house. The whole place was littered with old stones, parts of the broken roof beams lay scattered around. Observing all this, one would easily think it was a burnt-down house. Hence, fearing snakes and various other such dangers, people never set foot in these parts as far as possible.

Sanjay said, 'This kind of setting makes it much easier for us. Or else we might have been spotted by people at any moment, and then it would have been difficult to carry out the party's work.' Sanjay sat with his legs stretched out. He lit a cigarette. Nripen and Rajiv sat with their backs against the wall, their heads slumped. Rabin still appeared excited, his back erect, arms crossed over his chest. He paced up and down. A candle burnt in the room. Taking a couple of puffs of his cigarette, Sanjay turned and looked at Rabin. He said, 'Rabin, you don't look normal at all. That's not good in such work.' Hearing him, Rabin suddenly stood still and then he again began walking briskly around the room. Even though he thought of saying something, he didn't. Then, after pacing some more, he came and said, in a dreamy voice, 'The man tried to clutch the earth with his hands as he fell.' Sanjay took another couple of puffs of his cigarette. A jackal howled nearby, from the fringes of the orange-berry jungle. Then it stopped. Everything was silent.

Rabin was pacing across the room. The sound of that – in the midst of the stillness, only that sound resonated, it rang in the four hearts. Rabin clutched the hair on his head with his left hand, then released it. He clutched it again, released it again. Once again that dreamy tone came from his lips, 'The man didn't realize my intention even a moment before he fell.' Sanjay's head was slumped, he lit another cigarette. He didn't raise his head. In the brief light of the matchstick, his head had a reddish cast. And then there was silence. Again there was the sound of feet pacing. It beat loudly inside the four hearts. Blowing out a lungful of smoke, Sanjay saw that the candle was almost finished. After this we'll have to sit in darkness, he began to worry.

After a while, Nripen moved. He lifted his head slumped against his chest. He saw the candle was almost burnt out, its smoke ascended a little and dissolved into the darkness. As he watched, he wondered what time it was. He flung the question at Sanjay. 'What's the time now, Sanjay da?' Sanjay coughed a little, cleared his throat and said, 'I think it's past twelve.' 'But the last train hasn't gone by yet.' 'Then there's still some time left.' Once again, everyone fell silent. As if whatever there was to say had been said. The last dregs of the candle burnt now. Smoke rose. Rabin paced, the sound of it audible. Nripen saw all this, heard it. And as he did so, he tried to act normal, he tried to speak. 'Was he supposed to arrive before twelve?' 'That's what I had heard.' 'But we still have to wait.' 'By the way, is he coming from Calcutta?' 'I don't know for sure.' 'Will he come here?' 'We've been asked to wait here.' Nripen fell silent. He again dropped his head to his chest, but before that, he saw the candle burning, the smoke ascending and dissolving into the darkness. Sanjay flicked away the cigarette butt to the corner of the room. The fire's red was visible in the darkness. Sanjay continued to observe it. He saw that when that red was finally extinguished, the speck of space was filled with darkness. He looked at the candle. He saw that the flame of the candle wasn't exactly red, it had a whitish tinge. This little bit of light in the room could not be retained for much longer. He looked at the others.

Rabin continued to pace through the room. He was very childish. He had fulfilled his first responsibility all right, yet he was childish. He was uneasy staying silent like this. Sanjay tried to look at his face. It wasn't visible. Even if it was, it couldn't be recognized, even if it could be recognized, one couldn't exactly comprehend anything. He decided to speak. He said, 'Rabin, what are you thinking about?' Rabin slackened his pace, he looked towards Sanjay and said, 'Sanjay da, can I ask you for something?' 'What?' 'A Charminar.' 'But you never smoke!' 'Feel like smoking.' Sanjay took out a cigarette from the pack and gave it to him, took one himself and lit them. Rabin sucked inexperiencedly at the cigarette. He coughed. 'Charminar is a very strong cigarette, not everyone can smoke it.' Rabin didn't say anything. He took another puff. He coughed again. As he coughed, he looked at the candle. 'Sanjay da, the candle has burnt out, so what now?' 'Now darkness.' 'Do we have to wait like this?' 'That's what we've been told.' 'Sanjay da, I'm very tired.' As he spoke, he chucked the cigarette to the corner of the room. He clenched his hair in his fist. Sanjay did not say anything. He puffed at his cigarette. 'Sanjay da, it's getting darker and darker.' Sanjay took a deep puff of his cigarette. 'Sanjay da, the whole room will be dark very soon.' Now Sanjay raised his face. 'It seems like that initially, it's nothing.' Sanjay didn't say anything else. Rabin stopped his pacing and gazed at the candle's flame. Everything was absolutely still now.

Nripen and Rajiv sat with their shoulders hunched. Sanjay threw away his cigarette. In that desolation, Rabin gazed at the inside of the flame. As he gazed, he saw a rustic boy hunting birds with a catapult in the riverside woods. 'The man's chest had been pierced, blood gushed out and welled up and soaked the chest. For a second, I saw that, just before running away.' The shadows of the two men crouching enveloped their bodies. Sanjay's shadow was spread out on the wall. The candle burnt. Rabin was gazing inside the light. 'Do you know, Sanjay da, in my childhood, I wanted to write poetry.' Rabin paused. 'But of course, I didn't write any poetry.' Sanjay's face was turned elsewhere, he inserted his hand into his shirt pocket, took out the pack and from it a cigarette, lit it, then blew out smoke and said, 'You're still very sentimental.' At once Rabin retorted, 'Not at all! If that were so, I couldn't have killed the man like that and come away.' 'I compliment you for that. But you're sentimental.' 'Because I used to write poetry?' 'That too.' 'But at that age, all boys think of writing poetry.' 'No, not all boys, I didn't think of it.' 'You're special, Sanjay da!' Sanjay did not reply. He took a deep puff of his cigarette and exhaled the smoke. Once again, everything was silent.

Now the candle's flame flickered animatedly for the last time and then went out. Everyone, all four of them, saw the light dying. Nripen shifted a bit and said, 'It has become dark all at once. We have to wait in this very darkness.' No one added anything to that. A jackal howled again nearby. Nripen wondered what time of the night it was. He thought that the last train must surely have left, none of them heard it. This desolate, burnt-down house, not a soul around, no sounds whatsoever reach here, he thought. He tried not to think of anything. Here, in this darkness, in this wretched darkness, we must wait, just like this! Until he arrives. Perhaps all night. Perhaps until morning. Perhaps eternally. He would come, but we haven't been told where he was coming from. We haven't been told how he would come. He would deliver something to us. All very secret. We have to deliver that at a particular place. Rabin would leave with him. He would be in hiding for some days. Right now, it wasn't safe for Rabin to be in this area. In the darkness, Nripen brought his hand to his chest. Then he dropped his hand again.

Rajiv shifted about from time to time. He said, 'Terrible mosquitoes! Don't allow one to even sleep.' He clapped his hands and killed mosquitoes, there was the sound of that. He said, 'Got them!' From the darkness, Rabin asked, 'Are you sure?' 'Rajiv replied, 'Of course! I never miss.' Rabin said,

'Sanjay da, please give me the matchbox, I want to see the blood smears on Rajiv's hands.' 'It's not mosquito blood.' 'Then whose?' 'Your blood and mine. The mosquitoes sucked that.' 'Yes, that's true, that's our blood!' Sanjay said, 'You think too much.' Rabin replied, 'Yes, I'm terribly at fault.'

No one said anything after this. The four sat in the darkness. They thought. The mosquitoes multiplied in the darkness. The sound of mosquitoes flying. The sound of sitting in silence. Nripen placed his hand over his heart. 'As soon as it's dark, there are mosquitoes. And the mosquitoes are hell.' Nripen asked, 'How can you sleep in this situation?' 'Why, isn't darkness suitable for sleeping?' retorted Rajiv. Once again, there was silence. Nripen couldn't sit still. 'What time is it now, Sanjay da?'

'Whatever it is, we have to wait here, just like this.' All of a sudden, Rabin said from the darkness, 'When the man fell flat on his face, I felt like taking a handful of blood from his chest and looking at it, examining it. What's human blood like? How does it smell?' 'Then you'd die, you'd be caught for sure,' said Rajiv. Sanjay and Nripen didn't say anything. Silence for a while. The sound of heartbeats. The sound of mosquitoes. The sound of darkness. They could discern a kind of sound of the darkness too. And listening to that sound, they tired. Must say something. Their very existence now depended on the sound of speech.

After a while, they heard something that seemed to be flying all around them. A bat. The sound reverberated through the room. Rajiv exclaimed, 'Mosquitoes here and bats there! I'd kill the whole lot of them if I could!' Nripen asked, 'What would you gain by killing them? Bats have no blood in their bodies.' Rabin asked enthusiastically, 'Is that correct, Sanjay da? Don't bats have blood in their bodies?' Sanjay's voice revealed annoyance. 'I don't know.' Again, everyone became silent. Just the sound of the bat flying, just the sound of each one's breathing. And within that, after a while, everyone heard Rabin saying in that dreamy voice, 'But I know bats have blood. Because no creature survives without blood, it can't.' A jackal howled again. Rajiv squashed mosquitoes.

There was a muffled sound. A flash. Sanjay lit a match and lit a cigarette. Rabin's eyes were restless. Sanjay started thinking. And continued to think. It was definitely two or three at night now. He, the one who was supposed to arrive, had not come yet. He wondered what should be done about Rabin now. Gazing at the red flame of the cigarette, it struck him that Rabin needed some consolation. He took out another cigarette from the pack, thought for a while and then began: 'Rabin, would you like to smoke another cigarette?' Rabin initially mumbled a refusal and then said, 'Yes, give it to me.' Sanjay delicately held a light to the cigarette at Rabin's mouth. 'Puff gently, it's not bad even if it tastes bitter.' Rabin began to inhale. Sanjay looked at him in the darkness. Then he began, like a soliloquy: 'However free of blame we are individually, it won't do to think of a few people separately. Just think about it, and what's the conclusion about the whole world that you arrive at?' Sanjay paused in mid-flow, he saw Rabin puffing deeply, twice, on his cigarette. He decided to continue speaking purposefully, but before he could say anything, Rabin said, 'Do you know that song, Sanjay da, a wonderful melody the song has – "Bid me farewell once, Ma, I take your leave". What's the next line, Sanjay da?' Sanjay possibly felt annoyed at being interrupted. He said, 'I don't exactly know.' '"Laughing, I'll wear the noose, people of India shall see" – I think that's the line. Tell me, Sanjay da, the way people viewed Khudiram at that time, do people today view us in the same way?' Sanjay was getting irritated. He began puffing deeply on his cigarette. Rabin had thrown away his cigarette. The bat was flying around. If one strained one's ears, one could hear the sound of darkness too.

The desolation was exasperating, it was unsettling. Everyone understood that within, everyone felt it. But there was nowhere to go. Nothing to be done. He was coming, one had only to wait for him. All night long. All the while. Perhaps forever. Rabin sang softly in the darkness: 'Laughing, I'll wear the noose, people of the world shall see…' Then he changed it to '… people of India…' Rajiv was restless again. 'How can you sing in this darkness, Rabin?' 'But you're sleeping quite well.' 'Where am I sleeping! Mosquitoes…' 'And bats,' added Rabin. Then he continued in that dreamy tone, 'If these mosquitoes and bats unite and surround us, we can't escape. They'll suck our blood and finish us off.' 'You said it, mosquitoes and bats are frightful creatures in this darkness! They can easily suck the blood out of all of us.' No one said anything. Sanjay's cigarette was finished, he had thrown it away. Rabin didn't sing any more. He sat with his head tucked between his knees. He gazed… The boy tore off each page of his poetry notebook and floated it on the water. There were little waves in the water, the pages swirled, dishevelled, floated far away. The boy let out a deep sigh at that moment. Nripen shuffled again. From the darkness, a voice said, 'It won't be dark much longer, Sanjay da.' Sanjay did not say anything. Not eliciting any enthusiasm or response, Nripen became quiet. Once again, stillness filled the room. Only the sound of mosquitoes, the sound of the bat, the sound of darkness. Those sounds resonated in their hearts. Waiting. The waiting tolled bells in each breast. Sitting, waiting, the four men listened to that desolate bell's toll. Hearing, they sank into themselves. Sanjay thought, I'll have to keep sitting like this. I cannot violate the party's instructions. I have to wait even if it's forever. Can't afford to lose patience. He lit another cigarette. He tried to count how many were left. How long would they last? Sanjay lit a match. The matchstick emitted a sound in the depths of the darkness, it radiated a glow and then, once again, there was darkness. Waiting. Darkness. Outside, jackals howled again. The sound of a wild bird fluttering its wings. Nripen wondered how long this waiting would continue, how much longer they would have to sit like this. Sitting together like this in stillness was utterly pointless. It would surely be dawn shortly. Birds' calls soon. If one went outside, perhaps skylight would be visible in the east. A cool breeze. Perhaps the man we're waiting for won't come now. Though he is supposed to. Otherwise there is no point in waiting so long, mindlessly. Nripen put his hand on his chest once, he touched his face once, he made an attempt to sit in the room with his head hunched. This wait was most unsettling, most exhausting, most monotonous. After thinking for a while, Nripen was unable to think any more.

He asked, 'Sanjay da, shall I go outside for a while?' 'That's not very safe for us,' Sanjay replied. Rajiv again swatted mosquitoes. He thought, perhaps my hands are red with the blood of mosquitoes. In the darkness, the mosquitoes' blood would appear black. Bringing his hands to his nose, he tried to smell the mosquitoes, smell blood. They said the blood wasn't of the mosquitoes, but ours. Rajiv thought, the smell of blood that I get, it could also be the blood from our own bodies. Rajiv became irritated, 'Damn! It's meaningless to wait like this until eternity.' The whole night has gone by, the man hasn't come. Yet we're still waiting. Rajiv continued to think. Would have been better to have slept instead. But could one at all sleep with the torment of the mosquitoes? Sitting like that, with his head tucked between his drawn-up knees, Rabin sees the boy killing birds with a catapult. In search of birds, catapult in hand, the boy goes to the riverside. An ache emanated from Rabin's head and slowly spread through his body. He pressed his head between his two hands. Before entering the party, who was it who had said, 'You'll have to bear a lot of hardship – can you?' 'The one who can give up writing poetry can do anything!' Before shooting, Rabin had observed the man's face – exactly like his uncle. He hadn't been caught by anyone, he had fulfilled his mission safely and come away. Everyone in the party had complimented him. His uncle used to sit for prayers. There were plenty of pictures of gods and goddesses in his room. Durga's picture, Kali's picture, Shiva's picture. On one side of the door, a huge picture of hell. Different kinds of punishments for different kinds of sins – for stepping out of purdah, for foeticide, for cow slaughter, for killing men. Rabin tried to recall the images. Only darkness. The sound of the mosquitoes, the sound of the bat. The sound of darkness, penetrating the heart. Waiting, waiting eternally. He would come. Rabin had to accompany him. Perhaps there were bird calls outside. Everything felt discomforting. His head throbbed.

Sanjay lit a cigarette. For a moment, there was a flash of light on Sanjay's face, on his cupped hands. 'Sanjay da, please give me another cigarette.' Sanjay gave it to him. Rabin lit his cigarette from Sanjay's. Everything was unsettling now. This waiting, this blood, this darkness. As if there was no end to it. Rabin pressed his head with one hand. There was no relief. He looked at the cigarette's flame. This little point of light within the whole darkness. It had never struck Rabin earlier that there was such a similarity between blood and the colour of fire. With his right hand, he cupped his fist over the burning cigarette's head. Was his hand scalded? But he couldn't feel anything. At that moment, Rabin became desperate for a tiny bit of light. It was vital for him to see whether the palm of his hand was burnt black, or was red with blood.

*1970*

# Brothers Whitty and Shitty

Whitty and Shitty were brothers. They had no one they could call their own, except for a distant aunt. One day, even that aunt drove them away for not having studied and for going astray. In sorrow, Whitty and Shitty came and sat on the stump of the lightning-charred date tree. Lighting and puffing on a bidi that had earlier been extinguished after two puffs and tucked behind the ear, they decided: 'Can't go on like this, got to advance in life any which way.' But what should one do in order to advance? After all, advancing in life was not a trivial matter!

*Sexy kingdom!*
*Conclaves cackling!*
*The people all a-hush-hushing!*
*King and queen, elephant and horse –*
*All veils and deceptions!*
*Scion of the willing, minister's son,*
*All friends in league!*

Yet the people of this land did not get one square meal a day. It was difficult to get even a job washing soiled cups and dishes in hotels and restaurants, paying fifteen rupees a month. Apparently, many young fellows were sitting idle even after graduating in high-falutin' things like engineery. College graduates went around scalping cinema tickets. The boy who had achieved merit in the matriculation examination – hardly a couple of days later, he went around shouting in the middle of the marketplace, flag in hand: 'In this education system, the more one studies the bigger the idiot he becomes!' When this was the state of affairs, surely you couldn't advance simply by saying you wanted to advance.

Sitting on the stump of the date tree, legs crossed, puffing on a bidi, they wondered how to advance in life. Elder brother Whitty had always been a bit short of brains. He said, 'Come on, Shitty, let's get into trade.' Younger brother Shitty was quite cunning and clever. He said, 'Business? Where will you get the cash, pal? The capital will vanish and we'll sink by the day. Come on, let's raid rail wagons instead. Shibbu and company did just that and became millionaires.' Whitty wondered, with my ticklish hands and feet, will I be able to steal? But greed prevailed. Finally he decided – whatever has to happen will happen. Let's raid the wagons first! Must advance in life. That's absolutely vital.

A still night. Holding their breath, Whitty and Shitty crept along in the darkness, with utmost caution, to raid rail wagons. They saw a goods train standing on the tracks. It was night-end, fog all around, no one in sight in the vicinity. A long dagger in Whitty's hand. A hammer in Shitty's. Two sacks on the pair's shoulders. Shitty whispered, 'Come, let's strike this one.' He held Whitty's hand and moved ahead. Whitty's heart began to beat even faster. Life may end, but greed doesn't! After all, have to advance in life. Warily, cautiously, creeping ahead, they climbed onto the wagon. One pressed the dagger down forcefully on the hinge. The other began striking it with the hammer. Whitty was almost breathless with fear, joy and excitement. If they could break the wagon just now, they'd become rich! Wouldn't have to wander around searching for jobs in hotels and restaurants, paying a salary of fifteen rupees, washing soiled cups and dishes. Everyone would fawn over him, 'Why, it's Mr Whitty! Come, do come! Please sit down, have a cup of tea, a cigarette…'

While all this was being imagined, a man suddenly emerged out of somewhere, a Gandhi cap on his head, and grabbed their hands:

*Who's trying to be a man, sonny?*
*Raid the king's estate, do you?*
*Let's see the neck on those shoulders, honey!*

Now that's what you call fate! Wanted to become rich – and see what happened! The first day of setting out to make a living – and got caught! Whitty's face was quivering with fear. Slanting his cap, the man said softly in his deep voice, 'Wagon-breaking is a crime! You're antisocials! I'll hand you over to the police right now!' Hearing him, Whitty and Shitty became wide-eyed. Oh dear, what was to become of them now! Who would rescue them from this danger, who would give them courage, who would help! They poured their lives into entreaties to the gods. 'Oh Ma Kali! Oh Baba Tarakeshwar! We'll make you an offering of a pair of goats – just rescue us from this calamity, oh God!' They pleaded without restraint, tears streaming from their eyes. Perhaps, this made the gods merciful. In his soft voice, the man warned them: 'Sonny boys, don't run and flee, dear! Or else you'll be killed. Our fellows are just an arm's length away.' Whitty and Shitty had broken down completely. They dropped down to the pleats of the man's dhoti brushing the ground: 'Have mercy this time! Don't kill us, merciful father! Here, I twist my ear, I pull my nose, I'll never do this again as long as I live!'

It was as if the man was dying to be merciful. He removed the cap on his head and took it in his left hand. He smiled from the corner of his eye. Then he said, 'All right, we'll see about that. It's bloody cold! Come on, let's have some tea.'

So the man was not going to hand them over to the police! Whitty and Shitty simply melted. Oh, what magnanimity! What a great soul! Like grateful dogs, Whitty and Shitty began walking behind him. They went and sat down in a dark, shanty-like teashop. With the edge of the pleats of his dhoti, the shopkeeper wiped the dust off the bamboo bench for their benefactor. He greeted him unctuously: 'Ram Ram, Sethji, I'm honoured to ask you to sit.' The man ordered tea. Taking out a pack of expensive cigarettes from his pocket, he lit one for himself. Gave them too. Then sipping tea from the clay cup, he began narrating the real story. He took out a paan box from his pocket, put a leaf into his mouth, plucked out the stem, put some lime on it and put it back in his mouth, and then, slowly, gradually, began asking them about everything. 'Tell me honestly, sonny boys, why did you come to raid rail wagons?' By now Whitty and Shitty had melted with love and devotion. The person who could give them over to the police and have them sent to jail, why, here he was behaving so nicely with them! They babbled out, 'Swear to you, father! Today was the first time! Here, I twist my ear and nose, this will never happen again as long as I live!' Wiping his glasses on the folds of his dhoti, the man said, 'It's obvious that today was your first time. Nobody comes to raid wagons like this, at night, like thieves. Those who raid simply come during the day. They raid in broad daylight. And right in front of everyone. But why did you pick wagons, of all things?'

The light of dawn. In that light, the four gemstones on four of the man's fingers sparkled. Gazing at them in fascination, Whitty blurted out, 'Just to advance in life, sir! We didn't have any bad intention.' Hearing that they had set out like this to break wagons in order to advance in life, the man burst out laughing – *Ha ha ha ha!* After a round of laughter, he became serious. He said, 'Has anyone ever advanced in life like this, my friend? Can anyone advance in life this way?' Whitty and Shitty had begun to think that the man was God incarnate. But how else could they advance in life in these times of great deprivation? They pleaded with the man to tell them. The man removed the cap from his head and, as he folded it and put it in his pocket, he said, 'I can tell you the way. Accept it or not, that's up to you.' Then, clearing his throat with a cough, he said, 'It's precisely by things like breaking wagons that you should advance in life. But not like this. In daylight. Not like thieves. Bravely.' Hearing him, Whitty and Shitty were paralysed with fear.

*Build a shanty and try to live in peace,*
*But even here comes the king's sneeze!*

Went to break wagons once, and what happened? Got caught and almost got sent to jail! If any calamity occurs again… Almost as if he could read their minds, the man said, 'Don't fear! There's no danger. The policemen won't come. I'll explain all that.'

Whitty was confused: 'But raiding rail wagons is bad, a crime!' The man laughed again at Whitty's words. The four stones on his four fingers sparkled. He was expansive now. Patting them affectionately on their backs, he said, 'Damn it, sonny! Coming to break wagons with such notions! Exactly the opposite of what's to be said and done! Now there's the great Gandhi, such a big man! Come on, tell me, what lesson have you got from his life?' They stared blankly. The man said, 'The biggest lesson of the great Gandhi's life is this: that you never wear a cap, but make others wear the cap. Ever seen a picture of the great Gandhi wearing a cap? But those who go about practising Gandhism all have Gandhi caps on their heads. What you won't do yourself, you should tell others to do. What you can't do yourself, you must tell others to be able to do. That's the lesson of history. The real education. Understood anything?'

Unassailable logic. Whitty and Shitty listened. Slowly, the man explained everything to them. Five wagons of his goods were coming from Bombay. Expensive stuff. Worth a few hundred thousand rupees. Even before it reached the station, midway, he wanted to transfer all the goods into his own warehouse. 'No cause for fear. The train will move slowly. The wagons with the goods will be marked. Breaking the locks and taking out the stuff is all the work that is involved. A lorry will be ready under the rail bridge. The goods will be ferried away immediately. No need to be afraid of the police. A deal has been made with them. They will stand far away. There is a special arrangement with two rifle-bearing policemen. They will stand guard while the work is being done. If they think it appropriate, they may even sound one or two blank rounds.'

The man explained everything threadbare. He said, 'This is how you ought to advance in life. All the stuff is insured.' He would get back the value of the goods from the railways. And even before the train reached the station, all his stuff would reach his warehouse. Goods intact and money besides! And that is the way. It is precisely by such means that one advances in life.

The man was really magnanimous. He explained everything to Whitty and Shitty until it was as clear as water. He said, 'There's a little bit of risk in this work. But what's life without a little risk? Besides, such work is done only after tying up all the loose ends. There's no need to be afraid.' And if the work was accomplished, they would get something like ten thousand rupees in one go! Then they could sit at home for a month. Spend money freely. Drink booze, go to whorehouses. 'In this line, if you can take a little bit of risk, earning five-ten thousand rupees in one go is as easy as snuff! And if one can't earn five-ten thousand rupees in one go, then has one advanced at all in life?'

Another round of tea had been ordered for Whitty and Shitty. Sipping the tea, chewing biscuits, they reckoned it was just so that one ought to advance in life. It was like this that one hoodwinked people, making them wear caps while not wearing a cap oneself. In today's world, if you could not earn five-ten thousand rupees in one go, then, what the heck – could you call that advancing in life! They agreed. The gang of the man with the Gandhi cap would come tomorrow and impart to them all the methods and rules of working. They would accompany them to the railway sidings for a few days. They would teach them the use of all the special tools and implements, whatever was needed to break rail wagons. Remembering now that they had set out to advance in life by raiding wagons with a dagger and a hammer, Whitty and Shitty laughed.

But the story of Whitty and Shitty doesn't end here. There was a turnaround in the situation. Thousands upon thousands of drawn swords surrounded the royal court.

*The people raised a commotion:*
*'Listen, everyone, whose is this state so fine?'*
*All the leaders of the land claimed:*
*'Mine! Oh 'tis mine!'*

Then, one day, the Gandhi-cap-clad man arrived in the morning. He said, 'Hey, Whitty and Shitty! I'm in great danger! The red-flag chaps are really thrashing us. They're our enemy. Throw bombs at them. When you get a chance, slit their throats.' Whitty and Shitty had by then become very street-smart. They had learnt to figure out state politics. They began throwing bombs at the red-flag chaps. Whenever they got a chance, they went about slitting their throats. In the afternoon, Gandhi Cap arrived again. He said, 'The red-flag chaps are now our friends. Don't say anything to them. The blue-flag ones are bad. Our enemy. Throw bombs at them. When you get a chance, slit their throats.'

Whitty and Shitty then ignored the red-flag chaps and began throwing bombs at the blue-flag chaps. Whenever they got a chance, they went about slitting their throats.

In the evening, Gandhi Cap arrived yet again. He said, 'A compromise has been arrived at with the blue-flag chaps. The red-flag ones are bad. Our enemy. Throw bombs at them. When you get a chance, slit their throats.'

Seeing how things were going, Whitty and Shitty were struck dumb. Those who were friends in the morning became enemies in the evening! And those who were enemies were transformed into friends! 'Is this some kind of sorcery?' Gandhi Cap laughed. 'Yes, it's sorcery. This game has to be played like this.'

Whitty and Shitty understood everything. They sighed in realization. Things had indeed come full circle.

Then they finally stood up straight and told Gandhi Cap, 'Nothing more from us, find another way.'

Gandhi Cap replied, 'Beware! The writing on the walls proclaims: "Wagon breakers control Bengal's politics today!"'

They said, 'To hell with that!'

Gandhi Cap said, 'You're holding up advancement in life.'

They said, 'Let it get held up.'

Gandhi Cap said, enraged, 'For the last time, I tell you: think about it.'

They said, 'We've thought about it.'

Then Gandhi Cap made a sign. Those who practised politics with hoodlums had to keep other hoodlums to watch over those hoodlums. Two twin shots, four in all, were fired from within the darkness, tearing Whitty's and Shitty's lungs apart. Two or three droplets of blood splashed onto the clean, neatly pressed white khadi. Gandhi Cap immediately applied some lime on that. He placed the cap properly on his head. He strode ahead along the straight road. He had to join, just now, the rally demanding an end to the politics of violence.

*1973*

# Commentary '71

He was muddy up to his knees and his colour very tawny. He – the old bloke – had an amazing pair of cataractous eyes buoyant on his face, and muttered on indifferently. He said, 'Way back, in the riots of '47, my son was killed, and I've been searching for his bones ever since…' Around him were the sounds of the night. Kaath champa bloomed at the break of dawn. Its fragrance spread. The old man inhaled deeply and said, 'I think I smell something…' From desolate midnight roads came the whining of mongrel dogs. 'Who'll buy flowers? Who'll buy flowers? Jasmine, malati, fragrant bakul…' Crying, 'Why are you beating me? What have I done?', the octogenarian man fell flat on his face. Blood flowed on the street. Thrusting his bloodied hand into his trouser pocket, the youth rushed into an alley. The clerical worker hurriedly finished his shopping and moved away from the place without looking at anything. The old bloke gazed fixedly through his cataractous eyes and said, 'Will you hold my hand and just take me to the road, my dear? I want to search for my son's bones. He was killed in the riots of '47, on the streets of this very Calcutta.' The old man stood up, supporting himself with the help of his staff. His lips trembled with emotion. Inside the room, a blue light came on, someone binged all night. People moved aside, each in their own way. And on the vacant streets, the old man walked, tapping his staff. His eyes were cataractous, his face creased, his skin sagging. The old man walked alone on the open streets with the help of his staff. Those responsible for keeping watch kept watch in hiding. A few people silently played dice under the neon light, on spread-out newspapers. Shops and markets functioned as always. Vegetables were sold as usual in the markets. At the paan shop, a song from the film *Junglee* played on a transistor. The boy standing to buy cigarettes gyrated his hips. Paddy was harvested in the villages. In Vietnam, the liberation struggle continued relentlessly. American bombs rained down upon the hospital in the compound of the children's school. Petrified, the children screamed. 'Take shelter! Take shelter!' Only the old man's ears failed to hear the call to take shelter. All alone on the desolate streets, tap-tapping his staff, he advanced. His son was killed in the riots of '47. Now he wandered searching for his bones. With those very rheumy, cataract-afflicted eyes would he unearth his dead son's bones.

'What's the score today?' Two journalists sipped tea as they wrote newspaper reports. They exchanged gossip. 'Three people killed by pipe-guns in Beliaghata. One of them was dragged from a bus. A dead body severed into three pieces in Baranagar. And in civil-war-afflicted Shantipur, in

Nadia district, thirteen people were killed in an encounter with police. About ten people are in hospital. Curfew has been clamped on the entire locality. Only one statue's head has been broken – Rammohan's – near Howrah. My elder daughter's down with fever, she's been shitting the whole day. The wife's ill too, there's not a person at home to clean her up…' 'It's season-change time, brother, need to be a bit careful. Don't stay outdoors too late at night. Some positive things happening too. Do you know, after a single threat, a sixty-four-rupee doctor charged eight-rupees? The thieving traders in Burrabazar are losing sleep…' A blind beggar sat at a corner of the crossroads and sang, 'Mother's limbs burn away-ay-ay.' Darkness in front of his eyes, he had never seen anything until now, he was never going to see hereafter. Only that old man, with his rheumy, cataractous eyes, advanced. He was going to search and find his dead son's bones. There was no one in front of him. The streets were vacant. He was all alone. The solitary old man continued his journey on those vacant streets. Wind blew from all sides. The fragrance of flowers wafted by. The whispered conversations of frightened people. The song of the blind beggar: 'Mother's limbs burn away…' On one side, men were killed, and on another, sex-magazines cluttered the pavements. Who bought them? Two intellectuals walked by, talking about that. They smoked Charminars and discussed politics and society. Seeing people being nearly killed, they moved aside. They didn't want to get mixed up in any trouble unnecessarily. The tram clattered along on the road. 'There's no rationale for violence, shun violence!' Writing in yellow colour, written across cream colour, moved away from the front of the eyes. Every now and then the old bloke muttered, 'Way back, with the killing of my son, people began to be killed in this country. That trend continues to this day.' The old man's cataract-covered eyes sparkled. Darkness gathered in the nooks and crannies of the Maidan. In those patches of darkness, young men and women made love all night. There was a power crisis in the whole of West Bengal. All at once, a mass of lights went off. Scenting blood, a pack of hyenas stalked the dark streets of Calcutta. Thousands of manholes lay open. Preoccupied, inattentive pedestrians fell flat on their faces in all those places. The horns of ships blew incessantly from the Khidirpur docks. People walking by were startled. The sun's heat rose. Temperatures soared. Excitement grew in the city. There were killings in the morning. By evening, people forgot about them. Wiping away the bloodstains with their feet, mango-sellers lowered mango baskets there and sold mangoes at a rupee a kilo. People bought them. The sound of morning's bloodshed did not linger in the minds of the people in the evening. The blind beggar sang, 'Mother's limbs burn away…' The song floated around in the bosom of electricity-starved Calcutta. The song blended with the fragrance of flowers. Blended with fresh blood. With that smell, the newborn child suddenly whimpered in his mother's lap. The old man who was about to be murdered wanted to know: 'Why are you attacking me? What wrong did I do?' Driven crazy by that smell, the old bloke with cataractous eyes emerged into the street. He searched for the bones of his son killed in the riots of '47.

On the streets, now there was darkness in parts, and in other parts, vapid moonlight. In that light, people's faces could not be recognized. Through that, in solitude, the old bloke stalked the streets. Leaning on his staff, the old man advanced, his eyes cataractous. The roads were desolate. A few tall buildings touched the sky; some decrepit, rugged slums. From the darkness, every now and then emerged the cry of 'Hari bol, Hari bol'. According to custom, dead men rode on men's backs. Puffed rice and coins were sprinkled ahead and behind. Male and female beggars from the pavements raced and picked up the coins. A surly dog slept beneath the lamp-post. Its skinny puppies, their bones sticking out, roamed here and there. Every now and then, the lights-out siren sounded suddenly. The fragrance of kaath champa wafted from across the wall. The old bloke trudged the streets. He crossed the major streets and reached narrow lanes. Moonlight sometimes shone bright before his eyes, sometimes there was darkness. The old man crossed the rail tracks. On one side, there was a red light signal, on the other side a green one. He crossed the canal and the river. There were waves on the river, and boats, their sails unfurled. In solitude, the old man walked, leaning on his staff. Given his cataractous eyes, he walked on surmise. There were fields on both sides of the old man now. Farmers tilled the fields. Seeing the old bloke all alone on the road, they were curious. Where was the old fellow headed? 'I'm going to search for my son's bones.' They said, 'In these bad times, aren't you afraid to be all alone on the roads?' Shaking his tawny beard, the old man laughed. He didn't speak. 'Do you know there were seventeen murders yesterday?' The old man smiled wryly. He said, 'Wa-ay back in '47, it all started one night...' Seeing him mutter, people thought he was mad. The old man sang to himself, 'Mother's limbs burn away...' He walked the roads single-mindedly, taking small steps. No one accompanied him. Neither ahead nor behind. As he walked, he thought: surely one day I'll find the bones I'm searching for! All around him, people moved away. Those who had kept watch so long went away unworried. Under the neon light, on spread-out newspapers, a few people continued to play dice in silence. Night descended as usual on the streets of Calcutta. The preparations for murder continued. Packs of hyenas roamed around in the darkness. Manholes continued to stay open. People fell flat on their faces in the darkness. Before being murdered they screamed, 'Why are you killing me? What wrong have I done?' Wiping away fresh blood with his left hand, the mango-seller lowered mango baskets there and sold mangoes at a rupee for a kilo. People bought. The tale of the morning's killing became stale by evening. The solitary old man just walked on. Through darkness, through light, through vapid moonlight, he stalked the desolate streets. He said, 'It all began way back in '47...' Chewing paan, the newspaper reporters wrote reports of murders. They lit a cigarette to lend flourish to their language. They sipped tea. They drank coffee. In between, they shared confidences with the person beside. 'Do you know, Mukherjee, Haripada got his younger sister-in-law pregnant and while trying to get rid of that...' Red paan spittle trickled down the two ends of his mouth. At the paan shop, the song from the film *Junglee* played on the transistor. The youth jiggled his hips. Bombs rained on Vietnam. The patients moaned. In the children's school, the boys, unaware of anything right till the moment before dying, continued to recite catechisms. Every now and then, there were peace summits. In Delhi. In Calcutta. The tram with writing in yellow colour over cream colour went by. 'There's no rationale for violence, shun violence!' Litterateurs engaged in literature. Poets wrote poems. Teachers taught. Businessmen ran businesses. Vegetable sellers sold vegetables. Politicians did politics. Farmers cultivated paddy. In Rabindra Sadan, dance dramas were staged. But on the streets, in lanes and alleys, fresh blood continued to run. All that blood didn't dry in the sun. It didn't get washed away in the rain. Day after day, all that blood remained there, as a debt. Shaking his tawny beard, the old man said, 'Way back in '47, it began one night.' He said, 'Mother's limbs burn away…' He muttered and tramped the streets. In all the desolation, only that solitary old man walked the streets.

*1972*

# Bare Bones Awakened

It was morning when he got the news from a colleague. He said that a relative of his had given him an incoherent account of his narrow escape from Calcutta the previous night. In short, this is apparently what had happened. Around two in the morning, the waters of the Ganga suddenly began to froth. Most people in the city were in bed and knew nothing of what was happening. Their slumber was broken by a deafeningly loud crashing sound, accompanied by a flash of lightning in the southwest corner of the sky, the likes of which had never been seen before. At the same time, it became apparent that the city was flooding, with water levels rising up to the tenth floor. The people in the city drowned without knowing what was happening. The bearer of this news, who had escaped with his life, had seen the Monument crumble under the force of the water, crushing underneath it a much respected and well-known leader.

When he heard about the incident, it was too incredible to believe and, at first, he laughed it away. But later, after hearing about it from others as well, he was in doubt. Around noon, the news spread that Calcutta had apparently been destroyed in a terrible disaster. So many people were reporting the news that it wasn't possible to disbelieve it any longer. Besides, a few eyewitnesses had also been found – people who had been standing far away, or had somehow witnessed the incident from close quarters, or actually been in its vortex and yet been able to escape alive. Even though there wasn't much in common between the different accounts of the incident, he did not doubt that some kind of calamity had befallen Calcutta. He wasn't able to say with any conviction that the city was not wiped out as a result of the catastrophe. But his problem was that the accounts of the different people did not match in terms of specific events. They should have – and if they didn't, then one had to arrive at a different interpretation altogether.

The tale told by the three people who were now sitting in his room, extremely agitated, puffing at cigarettes, was even more terrifying. He had been prepared to hear a new version. Hence, although the events were shocking, he had not expressed any astonishment at all. When they first arrived, they were very bewildered. For the first few hours, they were speechless. Later, after some rest, a wash and some food, what they said was simply unbelievable. The three of them were friends. They were students at Presidency College and lived in a private hostel. On the day of the event – that is to say, last night – these three friends had been in the hostel. They had been chatting, they hadn't gone out because it had been raining heavily. Who likes to be confined like that in a room all day? Besides they were young fellows. Hence, at night – it was then approximately half past nine – after dinner, they felt a peculiar urge to go out. It was drizzling, besides nowadays it was quite unsafe to be out in the streets at night – though they seemed quite strong and capable in appearance. Nonetheless, these three friends decided to stroll around Sealdah despite the drizzle. They didn't have any particular objective as such, it was mostly out of a dislike for being stuck indoors all day. Then again, it was also a bit about challenging each other and wanting to vaunt one's bravado – no one wanted to lose to anyone else as far as courage was concerned. Be that as it may, when they got out onto the road, it was completely dark all around. It was drizzling, the street lights were out. The three chatted and joked – the way people of that age do, the things they talk about – and advanced towards Sealdah.

A little way before they reached the railway station, they heard a roaring sound that could only emanate from the throats of a vast multitude of people. Startled, they came to a halt. In their words, such a roar couldn't have come from less than a hundred thousand people. The dreadful sound continued as the assembled masses advanced in the direction of the city. They entered the city from wherever they could. Within a short while, they had occupied the entire city by sheer brute force. They – that is, the three youths who were eyewitnesses – thought that those who had come to take over the city were mostly Bangladeshi people fleeing the oppression of the Pakistani government. Some people from this side of the border had lent them active support and assistance, else they couldn't have occupied the whole city like this so easily, a city as large as Calcutta. And all three of them were unanimous regarding the immense bloodshed that had taken place. They said emphatically that some people, who were blinded by selfishness, who didn't give a damn about their suffering brethren from Bangladesh – whom they opposed – who sneered at everything, who said abusively that 'It's because of them, these refugees, that we're in this plight' – they were killed. Perhaps just a handful of them had somehow escaped from the city and survived. That was possible. What was more, these hundred thousand people from Bangladesh were so resolute and forceful that, in the space of merely a few hours of the night, they had entered and occupied the city's premier sites. They snapped all lines of communication with the outside world – which was why even twelve hours after the incident, people far away from Calcutta couldn't fathom exactly what had happened, what kind of an incident had taken place. In their – that is to say, the three youths' – view, they weren't content with merely taking Calcutta. Perhaps their aim was the whole of West Bengal. They were perhaps thinking about something like an undivided Bengal, combining West Bengal and Bangladesh, and, in that case, both the countries would be under attack very soon.

But the most astonishing thing about all this was that he had been to Calcutta only a fortnight ago and stayed there for a few days, and there had been no indication that something like this could happen, not the slightest hint. Unable to bear Yahya Khan's oppression, refugees had continued to pour into West Bengal. Their numbers grew by the day and had reached about seven million – this he had read and, having read it, just like others, he had felt a bit sad at that moment and then simply forgotten. He had not thought about it any more. Bangladesh was at war for independence. In the initial period, he had noted this with genuine enthusiasm and had been quite excited for the first few days. He had listened regularly to the news on the radio. He had been elated hearing about their victories. But, by and by, once things settled down and the stories in the newspapers stopped appearing on the first page and moved to the fifth page, he too had forgotten about the subject like everyone else – although it was quite clear that he had not wilfully done so, it was just the pace of the developments and the way it was presented in the newspapers that had made it so. Today, all of a sudden, the astonishing news of Calcutta being taken over by a huge army of refugees was utterly unexpected and even unbelievable. Could it possibly be true?

It was not just this one account or incident. Until this evening, he had heard lots of other things. Someone had said that last night everyone in Calcutta had seen an immensely tall man come walking from the northern sky, a red lantern slung on his hand. Seeing this, the people of Calcutta, especially those who lived in tall buildings and those from whose houses the sky was visible, got an inkling of some impending calamity. Someone else, quite elderly, whose two brown eyes were still dilated with fear, had somehow managed to escape and finally breathed in peace here. He said that, two days ago, he had gone to offer prayers at Pir Baba's dargah, and it was there that he had heard that Calcutta's destruction was imminent – Pir Baba had calculated on his fingers and declared that the earth could not bear such a great burden of sin, and that because of this the entire city would be struck a fatal blow, and thus would proper punishment be meted out, in full measure. On the afternoon of the day of the calamity, the man had heard jackals howling in Dalhousie Square and seen a vulture sitting on the top of Writers' Buildings. Another man – he too was elderly – had about a year ago sensed that a disaster like this was going to occur in Calcutta because he had seen lightning strike the roof of the Kalighat temple. In this one incident alone he had found proof that in the dark depths of Kaliyug, the Goddess was not going to remain on earth any longer. She was leaving the temple and going away, and before leaving had intimated: 'I'm going, now you lot do whatever you have to.' He narrated his experience. It was midnight, he had not yet fallen asleep. Suddenly, a mighty gale arose from the north. And what a tremendous gale it was – the buildings, all the tall buildings in Calcutta, crumbled like matchboxes in that gale, and thus was the entire city of Calcutta destroyed. Calcutta was now a city of the dead, no living beings survived there, not even a single jackal or a dog.

Reflecting now upon the different accounts of the events, he tried to come to some rational conclusion, even though the whole affair was so perplexing and all the accounts were so contradictory. Reconciling all of them and arriving at a conclusion was very difficult, at least as of now. If it was held that a terrible flood had occurred in Calcutta, as a result of which the entire city now lay under water, in that event, even though the incident might be within the realm of natural possibility, it did not seem possible. Because even twelve hours after such a terrible natural disaster, neither newspapers nor television had broadcast an authorized account of the extraordinary events. Second, the reports of eyewitnesses lacked credibility. Could the entire city have been submerged by the floodwaters of a suddenly turbulent Ganga, causing the death of the entire population of the city? Surely this must be an exaggeration! And third, if there had been a possibility of the Ganga frothing up like that for some reason, then, in this age of science, that would surely have been known in advance and there would have been a public warning. Even though some things still happened, which science, despite all its powers, could not anticipate – such things were merely exceptions, and it was dangerous to come to a conclusion about something on the basis of exceptions.

If the issue of a flood was rejected, some other very natural occurrences which were described by the eyewitnesses had to be considered. Pir Baba's counsel, or the incident of a vulture sitting on top of Writers' Building, or the matter of lightning striking the Kalighat temple – even if these were accepted as natural events, they did not prove anything. Because Pir Baba's warning, or a vulture sitting on top of Writers' Building, or lightning striking the Kalighat temple did not amount to portents of Calcutta's destruction, even though they were not normal incidents and we did not usually see such things. Consequently, just because they were not normal, they worked on common people's minds and, as a result, their superstition-riddled minds made much of some very natural things. Hence, in order to know what exactly happened in Calcutta, all these incidents could be ruled out as irrelevant. But one reference which he still wanted to analyse without dismissing was the story of a very tall man appearing in the northern sky, a man who walked with a red lantern slung from his hand. It seemed that there was some meaning in this – of all directions, why specifically from the north, of all colours, why red? If only convincing explanations for all such questions were found, some clue about the whole thing might perhaps emerge.

If the references to a flood and some purely natural phenomena were discarded, another account remained, which could be looked at in relation to the disaster in Calcutta. What the three youths from Presidency College said – the arrival of refugees and their takeover of Calcutta; even though it might appear to be improbable, the possibility of it had to be scrutinized and evaluated. First, the number of beggars in Calcutta was a few hundred thousand. That they wandered around crazily in search of food, clothing and shelter was a well-known fact. With their combined strength – if ever their coming together really occurred – they could well occupy a city like Calcutta, and it would not be right to rule this out as impossible. In fact, about one hundred and fifty years ago, in 1830, the city's beggars had actually assembled at some funeral ceremony. According to estimates, they numbered about two hundred thousand and, eventually, not getting any food, they began to loot shops and establishments – proof of it was there in the 15 May issue of *The News Mirror*. The news had appeared thus: 'The mass of humanity spread across the city and, becoming enraged after two or three days of starvation, having repeatedly returned to hundreds of places out of a motive of feasibility; or alternatively, all the youths, distressed at being so starved, lacking livelihood or any means, possessing not even a penny, began looting all the shops. And wherever foodstuff was available, they grabbed it. Then there was a rumour among them that the government had ordered that they should take whatever life-sustaining goods they found anywhere. In reality, this order was false, but that only enhanced their lust for looting. Some people did of course obtain food, but the majority of them were almost famished to death.'

Since there are many more such proofs, not just this one, a normal conclusion could be arrived at: that the beggar class of the city – in a word, the destitute – nurtured in their hearts a revolutionary spirit, even though only a few of these people agitated and 'the majority of them were almost famished to death'. Now, if we add to this incident the question of life or death of the seven million people who arrived from Bangladesh – a figure which is continuously increasing – then the whole matter becomes very dangerous. Seven million people, helpless, lacking means, who had borne the trauma of the partition of the country, borne the oppression of the Pakistani government, and had withstood the terrible floods in East Bengal – when they, unable to bear the oppression of Yahya Khan's army, fled with their wives and children and crossed the border and saw that the Indian government had nothing for them apart from a fistful of compassion, then they could well have risen spontaneously in revolt. 'Dire consequences unless two and a half million refugees are removed within a month' – when the newspapers publish reports with such headings, when they say that a few hundred thousand refugees 'are living under the open sky, in some places in knee-deep and elsewhere in waist-deep water, an indescribable plight after the last few days' heavy rain' – it is not impossible for them to revolt. And if they are joined by the local populace living on pavements, under trees, in motor garages, inside seventy-two-inch pipes, and beggars living like jackals and dogs, then it is not impossible that a city like Calcutta could be taken over.

But here, along with various other questions, one question assumes great significance, which is: how was this revolt accomplished in one day? If it is held that it didn't happen in one day, that it was in preparation for a long time, that some recent events merely added fuel to the fire, then the question remains: how did no one ever come to know about such a major underground movement, did not have the slightest inkling about it? Not even our police's criminal investigation department – how is that possible! Therefore, even if there was a probability of the whole thing happening, it remained unbelievable because there was no preparation for such an event, and no incident of this nature was known to have occurred in history without preparation. But if someone said there were preparations, that they had been going on, and, because we did not exercise our eyes and ears in the course of our daily lives, we were unaware – some might well contend so – then the present improbable situation becomes definitely possible and there is no option but for us to confront a terrifying future.

*1971*

# Feeling Distant

*Elena: Are you a revolutionary?*
*Sergio: What do you think?*
*Elena: I think you aren't a revolutionary, not even a counter-revolutionary, you are nothing.*
*Sergio: Then what am I?*
*Elena: Nothing.*

– T.G. Alea
from the film *Memories of Underdevelopment*

## ONE

At dawn, after nightlong dewfall, the Choudhuris' tin roof glistened like a silver sheet in the moonlight. At the banks of the large lake, fish found their way to Patit Paban Choudhuri's buoyed nets. Patit Paban squatted on the platform and hauled in the catch to the bank. It was the month of Poush. The smell of dumplings wafted in from the next house.

Grain-gathering girls stayed up all night, dreaming of that fragrance. Extraordinary dew, like an unseen hand, poured down relentlessly on the Choudhuris' five granaries.

Using rice paste dissolved in water, the peasant's daughter tried to draw the goddess Lakshmi's footprints across her courtyard, her alpona smudged by tears. Last night, her father had been taken away on the pretext of trespassing on the landlord's land. Pressed close to her, the younger brother pestered his sister: 'We'll get the fine-rice dumplings today, won't we, Didi, with grated coconut?' Wiping her tears with the palm of her left hand, the peasant's daughter consoled her innocent little brother. A raven cried *ka! ka!* inauspiciously from a branch of the shirish tree in the courtyard. Going to shoo it, she stumbled and stubbed her toe and caused blood to spill.

## Two

There was a dog show at the Maidan. He and I went there. Shiny cars, sparkling women. A winter's evening. I wished I could drop a mouse inside the suits of a couple of gentlemen. That didn't happen, found a girl. Light fell on the girl's bosom. Didn't see her face, didn't get the chance and didn't think about it either. I said, 'Give a lot of sex, do you, sis?'

'I don't.'

'Come along with us?'

'For free?'

'No. Treat you to phuchkas.'

Ultimately, it was settled on breast cutlet. We fed her breast cutlet, she kissed us.

She said, 'But I'm not in the trade.'

I said, 'Neither do we go pleasure-cruising accompanied by our wives.'

The girl went away after finishing her work and stood behind a lamppost. We crossed the thoroughfare and entered a side street. We walked by a shoe store and a liquor store. I remembered I had to buy shoes for Eva this month.

He said, 'Country spirit?'

I said, 'That'll do.'

We sat on a bench and drank from clay cups. An old fellow with a pointed beard was also drinking, the end of the pleated folds of his dhoti over his shoulder. As he drank, he sang to himself, 'O mother, how long will you make me-ee-ee wander?' Tears flowed down the old fellow's sunken cheeks.

## Three

In the morning, we found our pussycat lying dead in the veranda. Eva hadn't let me sleep until quite late last night. Mid-morning, when weak sunlight streamed into the room through the window, Eva pushed and pinched me. The sound of pouring water floated in from the bathroom. Rintu and Fintu learnt the alphabet: 'C-a-t spells cat, cat means beraal.'

Eyelids locked in sleep. I bought all the balloons from a balloon vendor at the Chowringhee crossing and standing there, all night long, burst them one by one. Eva pinched me hard and said, 'Come now, don't be so lazy, what will they think? Do you know, our pussycat died last night.' In front of my eyes, Eva's just-bathed face, wet hair spread all over her back. Today, I'll buy a whole lot of balloons and burst them one by one all night long. Burst them, but the pussycat – our pussycat died last night. Who loved the cat more – you or me or Rintu and Fintu?

Baba was sitting in the room upstairs, reading the newspaper. Dada must have left for the factory.

Rabindrasangeet played on the radio: 'Look how the morning star casts its eyes and gazes…' I wanted to laugh out aloud. I wished I could draw a cross with black pitch diagonally across the sparkling white walls of the orderly room, over that a skull, and in big bold letters write '440 volts, Danger'.

Eva hummed that stanza of Rabindrasangeet: 'Look how the morning star…' I gazed at Eva.

## Four

Although the bed she lay on was in darkness, she recognized the man. The man groped and moved towards her. She wanted to say, 'No… no…' But no sound left her throat.

She saw that groping paw coming her way, the face obscured by the hand. Somewhere, with a crash, a big lump of clay was rolled into the water. A wave arose, ripples. Trembling ripples, and finally everything subsided. Fish were caught in landlord Patit Paban Choudhuri's nets. The peasant's daughter tripped and spilt blood all over the courtyard. The plain fragrance of sojney flowers flowed in, relentlessly, from across twenty years.

## Five

As there was no light, everything was hidden. In that obscurity, they removed their masks and descended into the darkness, exposing their big teeth. Sniffing, smelling, sometimes groping, they probed that forbidden existence. Somewhere far away, within the mist, a lamppost would be lit. Somewhere, sacred texts would be recited, of the Buddha, of Jesus, of Mohammed. Disembowelling, tearing to shreds, taking in fully the smell of flesh and blood. Every now and then, looking around warily for whether anyone is watching anywhere. Being assured, fangs and claws are lowered again, and tear the stomach out from the abdomen. It gets bloodier. Ripping flesh with fangs and claws, attaining supreme contentment, they did their work under cover of darkness.

None of those who had gone ahead had returned. The whole place was desolate. And there were a few beggars under the tree, with a broken clay pot on the fire made of straw and twigs, old cabbage leaves cooking. A swarm of half-peeled, dry faces encircled them.

## Six

Eva wanted many things. A green field, a refreshing lake of clear water, a jamrul tree on which squirrels would scurry. A mud house, togor and balsam blooms sprawling over the courtyard. And if at night, in the fluttering breeze, the fragrance of kamini flowers wafted in – then nothing like it!

Eva was now dressing up. She looked at herself in the mirror. She would emerge fully adorned, proud. Eva wanted people to look at her, wanted to be desired. She felt happy when people gaped at her on the streets. The cigarette scorched my fingers.

When the taxi stopped in front of the bar, Eva got down. The neon lights of Park Street sucked away the night's darkness. A pleasing soft light in the room, no brightness anywhere to dazzle the eyes. I sat down with Eva. A uniformed waiter brought two drinks. I discerned the smell of my own blood in that coloured liquid. Eva became sharp-eyed when she drank alcohol. I gazed at her. The cigarette burnt out in my fingers.

## Seven

At the Choudhuri family's senior section's granary, dew fell all night long. Eva and I sat and merrily, smashed glasses one after the other. The shards of glass were strewn all around and gradually became a city of mirrors. 'Oh dear, what's to become of us now?' said the peasant's daughter as she sat down. Blood spilled on their courtyard. Eva clapped her hands in joy. The old chief rent-collector, fixing the strings holding his spectacles around his ears, his body bent, recited in a mutter, 'This time, the collection's very bad, young sire, the peasants are agitated.' On Park Street, the clatter of glass shattering. Eva giggled, *hee hee!* She says, 'Isn't my laugh like Gina's?' Plastered on alcohol, Louis XVI says, 'Who's asking you to eat cakes instead of bread – it's bread you shall eat, got it?' Broke more glass. All around the room heaps of broken glass. And as my own distorted image flashed in that broken glass, raising my arms, I, a member of the family's junior section, thrown into a frightful confusion, flailed my arms in self-defence. When the waiter came and enquired, I screamed out, 'How late is it?'

There was no reply.

## Eight

By and by, the street becomes quadrangular. Negotiating the twists and turns becomes increasingly complicated. Shona boudi lies wearing Eva's skin. He sees a feudal, bluish hue oozing out of the blood. The owl hoots from inside the alcove. The light comes on instantly. I see Shona sprawled across the couch, giggling – *hee, hee!* When Shona pulls a long face, the light will go off. In consternation, Babu dada would go and stand at the street crossing, puffing on a cigarette. Flapping its wings, the owl will emerge from the alcove and sit on Shona's shoulder. Babu was very angry about the owl: 'I'll kill it one day!' Shona: 'Oh let it be, the innocent creature, doesn't harm anyone.' Babu does not reply, he merely grinds and gnashes his teeth and goes out to the street crossing.

Suddenly, the door opens. The interior of the room is visible. But nothing can be seen. Babu hides everything that belongs to Shona. Sure enough, one day, as she sleeps, he sneaks out and… Shona's…

## Nine

He searched for matches, couldn't find them. Went to the bathroom, vomit poured out. Washing his hands and face with water, he recovered somewhat, and as he was about to go back the mechanical bird called out.

There is much more on the alcove. A bottle of perfumed oil, a powder-box, hairpins, a golden lipstick tube. In one corner, the mirror. The sindoor-box, a packet of incense. Beneath the upturned stool, the mechanical bird. The bird speaks. Pecks and chomps audibly at grain. Sometimes, it nibbles. When it is annoyed, it comes to peck. And at night, it becomes an owl. He looked up and saw the picture of Goddess Lakshmi overhead. Lakshmi worshipped by two generations. Eva performs her puja. A garland of marigolds on the picture. The couch spread across the room. Covered with a white sheet. He tore the garland and threw it to the ground. He brought down the picture carefully. The picture preserved by two generations. He wondered where he would keep it. Unable to decide, he put it down on the alcove, near the mirror, where the owl sat, the mechanical bird.

## Ten

All the peasants went home. All the labourers, all the scholars. Only he remained, just him. His body got wet in the rain. Warm in the sun.

His colour drained away in the swampy forest's mud and slime. What happened to you, what happened – you wanted to live! But what happened instead? Now darkness swung unevenly on the branches of the pakur tree. The moon floated wildly in the dark waters. The hoot of an owl rolls in from some fantastic forest clump.

The barrel of the gun is laid on the chest. He screams, 'This land is ours. The fragrance of dry earth moistened by rain is smeared over our body.'

## Eleven

Somewhere in the vicinity of this city, there's an empty field, there are trees somewhere, where birds dwell. Morning dawns to birdsong there. As he thinks along these lines, he sees water overflowing in the bathroom. He doesn't hear anything. Walking through the mists, treading through many fields, woods and forests, he finds the prayed-for dawn.

## Twelve

Nobody gives us anything, we snatch it away.

*1969*

P.S.

Insights
Interviews
& More...

## Who is Subimal Misra? Why is he an 'anti-establishment' writer?

## Subimal Misra on Subimal Misra

‘’

I was born in a poor brahmin-pandit family.

*My birthday*

I do not know the precise day I was born. My mother told me I was born on a Wednesday in December 1943. My ‘official’ birthday, 20 June 1943, is entirely fictitious, ascribed by the school I was admitted to. I was born in a poor brahmin-pandit family. Like in all the poor families of my village, there was no custom of remembering or celebrating the birthdays of children.

*About me*

I got an MA in Bengali from Kolkata University but never completed my thesis. I gave up a college lecturer's job in a mofussil area since the teachers spent most of their time playing cards. In the honours class, there was just one girl, who sat demurely. Besides, the police were after me, partly on account of political suspicion. Far away in the mofussil area, I missed Kolkata terribly. I could not stay beyond three months, and I returned to Kolkata, my beloved place of work.

I destroyed all my academic records.

I was a humble school teacher in a high school in Kolkata. Here too, my salary was not raised as I refused to appear for the B.Ed examinations. Besides, I had destroyed all my academic records. The school was adjacent to Sonagachhi, the city's most renowned red light area. A large section of students from that area (most of whom did not have a father's name) came to study at this school, and I, like other teachers, had to invent names for their fathers. Through my relationship with the students, I was able to gather information and hard facts about the crude and naked business system, where a son is often deputed to bring customers to his mother. I have depicted those grim pictures in some of my writing.

I live in a small, untidy rented flat, crowded and littered with thousands of books of all descriptions, records of Indian and Western classical masters, empty tea cups and cigarette packets, leaving little or no space for movement. I am married and have a daughter, my wife visits me occasionally. In my family life, I maintain the spirit of living together, and let my wife lead her own life without any complaint. I usually do most of the household chores as my mother is extremely old and the maidservant often prefers not to come.

I live in a small, untidy rented flat, crowded and littered with thousands of books.

### *A different writer*

I am not a 'good' writer or a 'parallel' writer, but a *different* kind of writer. What's understood to be story-writing – I don't do that. I destroy that. From the very beginning, I wanted to depart from the conventional narrative tradition that defines all writing.

I am not a 'good' writer or a 'parallel' writer, but a *different* kind of writer.

My writing has the capability to challenge world literature in some aspects. Subimal Misra has no earlier parallel.

My writing has the capability to challenge world literature.

***Use of montage***

I tried to bring the montage technique of cinema, specifically Eisenstein's, to language and writing, so that two or more visual elements are brought together to produce something new.

In 'Haran Majhi's Widow's Corpse *or* The Golden Gandhi Statue from America' (1969), I tried to go beyond both the narrative as well as the documentary form. Employing Burroughs's *cut* method, I searched for a new third form, which could bring to writing the language of cinema, specifically the montage technique. The result was something new in the context of Bengali literature, and also perhaps in writing in English. 'Haran Majhi…' could be called a work of magic realism.

I searched for a new third form, which could bring to writing the language of cinema.

Let me give an example from Italian neorealist cinema. In the film *Bicycle Thieves*, there is a scene where the poor father and son are eating, and two wealthy people are also eating nearby, and the little boy stares at them. These two contradictory things, composed within the same scene, produces a third dimension. It is not read, it is not a statement. It is something ephemeral. It is a sense, where the observer or reader is also a part of the process.

The very title, 'Haran Majhir Bidhoba Bou-er Mora ba Shonar Gandhi Murti', that is, 'Haran Majhi's Widow's Corpse *or* The Golden Gandhi Statue', brings together two completely different, incompatible entities – the corpse of the dead widow of a peasant from Bengal and the father of the nation and national icon, Gandhi.

Later, I also attacked the montage technique; for instance, in the story 'Sotityo Ki Rakhbo, Aparna?' ('Shall I Retain My Chastity, Aparna?', 1985).

> I have written on specific subjects and themes, where *the way of saying* is what is said.

### *Way of saying*

I have also written on specific subjects and themes, where *the way of saying* is what is said. I do not believe there is such a thing as 'reality'. 'Socialist reality' too has been attacked. In the recent story, 'Mati Norey' ('The Earth Quakes', 2005), while talking about my youth, I confront a wrestler. This is an allusion to a famous, popular writer. I wrestle. I myself do not know whether I win or lose. The ground beneath my feet quakes. It is about wrestling with popular writers.

> I do not believe there is such a thing as 'reality'.

### *Against the commercial*

As a writer I have always been against commercial writing, which enables readers to effortlessly swallow what's written. I have never written like that.

After writing for over forty years, I have not allowed a single word of mine to be published in commercial publications – those that can bring fame and money – even after being invited to contribute. I do not want to write for publishers who pay because I do not write what they think can sell. If they did publish my work, I would have to compromise. I only write for little magazines. When I get invitations to write from both establishment and little magazines, I always go for the latter. If popular writers are writing in a little magazine, then I don't write for them. I have not permitted my stories to be used in commercial theatre either. An invitation from a commercial magazine or publisher is an insult to my writer-self. I fear I have not been writing anything 'new' or controversial. Little magazines have limited circulation. They are unable to pay their writers. Hence, I have never earned any money from writing.

I do not want to write for publishers who pay because I do not write what they think can sell.

I have never earned any money from writing.

*Bengali publishing*

People in Europe, who read books by European writers, can never understand the problems facing a serious writer in a language like Bengali. There are publishers for non-mainstream writers there. Such publishers do not exist here. How a writer like Subimal Misra struggles against market forces and lives his anti-establishment writing practice – Europe can learn about and from that.

In the Bengali publishing world, only those books are published which can sell well and yield a profit to the publisher. Hence, publishers want to publish those kinds of stories and novels.

My books do not have a specific price, they have very long titles, and publishers do not comprehend my 'anti-establishment' writing. Hence, they do not publish my work. They fear that the market cannot accept my writing. No serious writing in Bengali can be popular today. There is no publisher in Bengal who has the capability to publish my writing.

For instance, they do not understand that I try to communicate through the very letters themselves. There is almost no press in Kolkata that is willing to do the kind of typographic work I want.

But I write, so what am I to do after that? Because I write in such a publishing context, I have had no option but to publish my own work. But I do not have the means to do that. I was a humble school-master. Because I did not take the B.Ed degree, my salary was not raised. As a matter of principle, I did not teach tuitions. Hence, there was no possibility of accumulating money except by saving. By cutting down on all my requirements, like getting by without eating fish, I saved money. I even had to take a loan at an exorbitant rate of interest from the watchman at my school.

' '

No serious writing in Bengali can be popular today.

I try to communicate through the very letters themselves.

However, some of my readers wished to pay more than the suggested price for my books, they argued with me to let them help. That is how I brought out my books. I do not make any costly covers, I use cheap paper.

No book of mine – not a single one – has been reviewed in all these years in any mainstream publication. How is this possible? My writing has simply been ignored, concealed and denied by the Bengali publishing world, the totality of it, which does not permit someone like me to even live

No book of mine – not a single one – has been reviewed in all these years in any mainstream publication.

***Books versus commodities***

How are my books to be sold? Bookstores sell commodities called books and, hence, Subimal Misra's books are not available in bookstores. I have no desire to be read by one and all. That is impossible.

Bookstores sell commodities called books and, hence, Subimal Misra's books are not available in bookstores.

The print-run is small. Each book has a personal touch, rendered by me by hand. The books often have very long titles. One of my books does not even have a title – it has a number of suggested names and the reader can tick the one he prefers.

The book-sellers in College Street don't keep my books. So, besides writing and publishing, I also sell my books by myself. I work on each and every aspect of the book, from writing to text composition, layout, cover design, printing, conveyance, storage, distribution and sale. In this way, I have sought to demonstrate my opposition to the whole commercial publishing industry and practise an alternative.

There is no means of promotion for someone in my situation. Some little magazines carry advertisements of my books. But there are a few readers, I know that, and I try to reach them. Most readers find out about my books by themselves. They live in mofussil areas. They write to me or call and request that I send them my books by post. I have been at the Kolkata Book Fair with my books from the very first fair. I meet my readers there. I like to talk to them, as I empathize with such people more than with the 'smart' folk of Kolkata, I can understand their humble circumstances. So I'm prepared to give away a book for even a rupee.

I sell my books after a discussion with the buyer. My books do not have a price; there is a suggested exchange amount, or *whatever a Subimal Misra reader thinks the exchange amount should be.* A reader without money can get a book for a token payment of one rupee. On the other hand, someone I do not want to give the book to cannot get it even if he pays a thousand rupees. If a buyer is dissatisfied with the book, he can get his money back.

Quite a lot of sales take place at the fair. When the buyer puts the book in his bag and

I have sought to demonstrate my opposition to the whole commercial publishing industry and practise an alternative.

My books do not have a price; there is a suggested exchange amount.

says, 'Now no other book shall enter this bag' – that's my reader, that's my reward. It is thus that I have been able to maintain my identity as a writer.

It is not a question of what I write but *why* I write, why I am *anti-establishment*.

### *On being 'anti-establishment'*

There is a larger 'system' within which one lives and writes. When one speaks about an *alternative* system, our narration must also be different – the thinking, the way of thinking, all have to be different. It is not a question of what I write but *why* I write, why I am *anti-establishment*. If writing is part of the establishment, then the very form of anti-establishment writing must challenge it.

Anti-establishment is not a solution in itself, it is a question – a serious one, which opens up new terrain or action or conception every day. Anti-establishment is not passive in character, it implies activity, active antagonism. Slogans and words cannot make one anti-establishment. Our life and the society are fully governed by the establishment, and therefore an anti-establishment writer cannot sit idle in regard to the various forms of the establishment – the family, religion, marriage, state, political parties, the set human relationships and obnoxious codes of conduct. He is a 'new' man, who is not ready to accept anything conditioned, who is always 'open' to new realities and ideas. Only when he is outside

Anti-establishment is not a solution in itself, it is a question.

of the realm of conditioned ideas can he perceive the reality.

An anti-establishment character is a man of new mentality, or as Marcuse said, a man of 'new sensibility'. To me, anti-establishment is not a programme of catchy slogans that will make me 'look' rebellious. The rhythm of the attitude has got into my very blood.

What can an anti-establishment character do, except attack this monster which eventually destroys all the finer elements of humanity? It is a desperate fight, as he who fights is also a part of that society. He aims to destroy all kinds of state-bourgeois ethics, lifeless but bright language and dirty thought patterns which are reactionary and based on commercialism. Anti-establishment stands against all kinds of commercial and bourgeois culture and entertainment which compel people to live in abominable conditions (both materially and spiritually) while offering a hollow aesthetic pleasure. In the same way, I also protest against the so-called proletariat literature and culture, which is nothing but a wrong interpretation – deliberate perhaps – of ideas. It is a kind of deviation, it is nothing but slavery to the dictatorial establishment.

The term anti-establishment has become cheap, its edge has been dulled through overuse. All around, there are hundreds of those who are anti-establishment, who dream of toppling the establishment. But the

An anti-establishment character is a man of new mentality.

The term anti-establishment has become cheap, its edge has been dulled through overuse.

establishment – that is to say, power – easily co-opts all such 'opposition'. On the other hand, the nature of the establishment is so multi-form, it changes itself in accordance with the times. The whole world has been transformed into an exchange-based market civilization, where everything is for sale and purchase, all human relationships, even the notion of being anti-establishment. I am not a marketable anti-establishment item. So, now, I must be anti-anti-establishment.

Expressing anti-humanism becomes a way to challenge the professed humanitarian attitudes of the establishment.

### *Man comes first*

To me, 'man' comes first and foremost. I do not mean 'man' in the sense in which the term is employed by political entrepreneurs of all parties, and the smug middle class, tucked away securely in the comfort of their homes.

It is commonplace now for writers to express humane concern and empathy for the underdog. That now forms part of the establishment. So that must also be challenged. Expressing anti-humanism becomes a way to challenge the professed humanitarian attitudes of the establishment.

I believe in using a kind of 'planned violence'.

I believe in using a kind of 'planned violence', as used by Truffaut, with all its implications.

For me, only that which is created by man is aesthetic. Marx's statement, 'Nothing human is alien to me', is very dear to me.

Reality – raw and cursed – is the thing that I want to project. To me 'reality' is not a fixed moment of the unchanging present. Reality is a dialectical situation, in between the past and the future.

There is nothing like the last thing or any absolute in literature. I will have to try to cross even the postmodern mark. If I cannot, then all my writing should be destroyed, there is no use for all that rubbish. I stand against myself, against all my creations. I reject everything, including myself, and thus I question. I hate stagnation of thought, ideas and beliefs. There are vast possibilities in front of us, new horizons, new understandings... Man cannot stop, man cannot brood over myths, he has only this option open to him – to move on, or perish.

To me, literature cannot be entirely based on situation or plot or character or theme. Creativity is apparently chaotic, impatient, detached and often without a definite end or solution. Here, affection, lust, hatred, compassion, brutality, love, humanism, everything gets mixed up and plays a definite role in shaping existence. It is, at the same time, subjective and objective, civilized and suffused with libido.

The main thing that prompts me to write is my curiosity about the complexities of life. I want to discover through my writing what life is, what lies behind a certain movement or action.

' '

I stand against myself, against all my creations. I reject everything, including myself, and thus I question.

I want to discover through my writing what life is, what lies behind a certain movement or action.

My query towards life and its possibilities, its various patterns and combinations, helps me. The best knowledge comes only through close contact with life itself.

Oppressed humanity is at the centre of my writing. When I see the helpless section of humanity fighting even a little against all the odds, I get a kick. Crude politics has no part to play in my writing. If there is anything political there, then it comes authentically from the attitude of the masses. I don't write from imagination, I collect material from around me, from the complex social order in which we live.

Oppressed humanity is at the centre of my writing.

***On middle-class mentality***

I hate the middle-class way of thinking, the thinking that perceives blood while looking at the lipstick on the wife's lips. I feel humiliated to be in the line of litterateurs like Rabindranath Tagore.

I feel humiliated to be in the line of litterateurs like Rabindranath Tagore.

Let people see the reality that I depict. Let them see their true situation themselves and shudder, let them ponder over their hypocritical social situation. The overturning begins when people develop the power to think, not merely through capturing political power. I want to take people to that level of realization where they themselves start breaking down their own situation. So far, the publishing process has had a form that to me appears extremely watery, sentimental and like a pathetic bleat. I want to stab people with my pen and I have to search for how to stab in my own way. I am not bothered about whether this results in literature or whatever else.

Left-wing literature is that which is not merely class-conscious but is more than that, which is the literature of class hatred. By reading this, the blood in the hearts of the bourgeoisie should turn icy. It cannot be part of pleasurable literature. It must always be destructive – and creative moments would arise from within this destructive explosion. We should not show optimism for any mechanical path. We must prick the syphilitic sores of this class-divided, counterfeit civilization until liberation is achieved. Reading such literature, people can decide for themselves which the correct way is and which is not. For this, imagination is necessary. It is this imagination that binds readers to literature. The left-wing literature that we wait for is the imaginative literature that inflames readers with class hatred.

Revolution is not a hollow sound. It is a creative process. Just as the footfalls of class struggle need to be made audible in literature, there is also a need to be creative. Because we are unable to bring these two aspects together, our so-called revolutionary writing becomes one-sided.

The very existence of the educated middle class depends on the poverty and lack

We must prick the syphilitic sores of this class-divided, counterfeit civilization until liberation is achieved.

Revolution is not a hollow sound. It is a creative process.

‘ ’

Middle-class values are the biggest impediment to social change.

I want to assault this value system, I want to rupture their rhinoceros-skins.

of education of ordinary people. They dream about juicy, bourgeois consumption. They pay lip service to communism while actually deriving contentment from considering themselves beings superior to labouring folk. These half-educated, half-penny wise men need to be exposed – for instance, when they squabble with a rickshaw-puller to reduce his fare, or bargain with a cobbler on the road.

Middle-class values are the biggest impediment to social change. We practise Marxism while retaining this value system, as a result of which a trade union leader has to go to Kalighat to offer prayers before a protest demonstration, or a nuclear scientist cannot but be a disciple of Sai Baba. I want to assault this value system, I want to rupture their rhinoceros-skins. Hence, I have to employ extremely offensive language. I do not think about the felicity of expression, I do not believe in that. I look at whether or not I am able to achieve my objective with the language. I want to attack in such a way that, seeing our own situation, we, the middle class, ourselves shall start destroying the rotten heap that our social system is. The next stage after this is definitely thought about, but I shall be happy if I can make this a sound assault. Therefore I do not have to 'make up' a Marxist story by placing the possibility of social transformation clearly at the end of the writing. If ultimate destruction is shown, then the desired construction becomes transparently clear.

*On Gandhi*

I do have a kind of Gandhi-fixation. He appears in the title of my first collection of stories ('Haran Majhi ...'). The white donkey in 'Money Tree' symbolizes Gandhi, in terms of purity as well as stubborn foolhardiness. Only a donkey would do all that he did for his countrymen.

' '

I do have a kind of Gandhi-fixation... Only a donkey would do all that he did for his countrymen.

*On sex*

I try to take sex away from the realm of mere sensory enjoyment. I use it instead to expose the shameful character of middle-class morality. The most sacred relationship between man and woman has been reduced to a mere commodity. Especially in my most recent writing, I lament this, I weep.

I use [sex] to expose the shameful character of middle-class morality.

*My stories*

To understand my stories, one has to go beyond the Bengali language. Just like in order to understand Joyce, one has to forget the English language.

I cannot describe my stories in simple sentences. They are complex and multi-dimensional.

*Ideal writer*

My ideal writer is only Subimal Misra. I also like to read Joyce, especially *Finnegan's Wake*, Kafka, Proust and also de Sade.

> What do I 'get' from this relentless rebellious attitude? I get nothing whatsoever.

### *Awards*

I do not believe in literary awards. A retort of Sartre seems to be very important in this context. Refusing to accept the Nobel Prize, he said that he would have also refused the Stalin Prize if it had been given to him. That had a major influence on me as that was when I began writing. The idea of the living practice of a writer, opposed to and attacking the system.

### *What do I get?*

I live in a tiny rented flat. My wife says that the money I have spent on my books could have fetched a nice, large flat in a posh locality of Kolkata. 'What has literature given you?' she asks.

What do I 'get' from this relentless rebellious attitude? In the sense of what 'getting' means in this commoditized civilization, I get nothing whatsoever. Simply walking endlessly is my gain and my pleasure. To go on examining myself relentlessly and to walk joyfully while examining myself. All that is held to be correct is what most needs examination. The line that I like most in what I've written – that is what should be deleted first.

> All that is held to be correct is what most needs examination.

### *On translation*

Rendering my work into English is very difficult. It is very difficult to grasp the anti-establishment character of my writing without knowing Bengali and about Bengali culture. Translation is therefore very challenging.

# Translating Subimal Misra's Stories

V. Ramaswamy

My friend, Mrinal Bose, a physician and writer, introduced to me the name of Subimal Misra in 2005 when I asked him to name one writer in the contemporary Bengali literary scene whose work he considered important. I said I would translate his writing.

Bose told me that reading Misra had always been a learning experience for him. He said he hardly read Bengali writers any more, yet he continued to read Misra. 'His glory is intact. His strength as a writer is his irreverent and blasphemous voice and his ruthless and uncompromising portrayal of our life and times.'

Bose gave me Misra's phone number a few days later. I rang up the author to express my intention to translate his writing and to enquire about getting his books. Misra directed me to a couple of bookshops in College Street in Kolkata and also to a publisher who had brought out compilations of his stories and novels. I followed this up immediately, and obtained whatever was available.

I began translating the first Misra story a couple of months later, egged on by Bose. I then telephoned Misra and told him that

Misra encouraged me in my translation effort and gave the project his blessings.

I had actually begun the translation and just completed one story. I sent this to him by post, as I did all the other stories soon after translating them. And thus began our relationship, or friendship. Misra encouraged me in my translation effort and gave the project his blessings.

Thanks to Subimal Misra and his friend Procheta Ghosh (Lala), who publishes and edits the little magazine *Jari Bobajuddhyo* (*Continuing Mute War*), I got most of Misra's published works, as well as writings about Misra and published interviews.

◆

Misra began writing stories in 1967. Among the varied influences he acknowledges are: Dostoevsky, for his mastery of narrative; Proust, for his distinctive style of writing; film-maker Eisenstein, for his montage technique; Joyce, whose *Finnegan's Wake* he regards as his favourite book; Sartre, for his political stance of refusing the Nobel Prize and emphasis on living practice; Samuel Beckett, especially his prose writing; William Burroughs, for his *cut* method; and film-maker Jean-Luc Godard, for his craft of making films a medium of argument. Among Bengali writers who have influenced him, Misra acknowledges Jagadish Gupta (a now-forgotten contemporary of the popular writer Sarat Chandra Chatterjee), Kamal Kumar

Majumdar and Amiya Bhushan Majumdar. However, despite these diverse and eclectic influences, Misra's writing is uniquely his own.

Misra's work has been conspicuously ignored by the mainstream Bengali publishing industry, the media and the literary domain. Consequently, his name is largely unknown even in Bengal. Neither are translations of his writing into English or any other language available to the wider world of literature. But unimpeded by personal penury and lack of recognition, reward or renown, Misra has simply written on – and thus kept alive and enriched the tradition of protest in Bengali literature. He is highly regarded by a small circle of readers in India and Bangladesh, especially in the domain of little magazines and parallel literature, including some acclaimed writers.

By his life choices – such as destroying his masters' degree certificate, or giving up a college lectureship and teaching in a school in Sonagachhi, Kolkata's infamous red-light district – and through his writing and self-publishing, Misra has sought to stand apart from the society around him. He critically interrogates every aspect of the relationship, through the printed word and books, between writer and reader and between writing and society, in a context of mass illiteracy.

Subimal Misra is like a secret cult in Bengali literature. And through the internet, blogs, Wikipedia and YouTube, Misra's readers have tried to make his name more widely known.

◆

That Misra was considered anti-establishment and experimental, had stubbornly shunned mainstream publishing and periodicals and disavowed copyright, made me interested in and curious about his writing. But once I began reading his early stories, I discovered an affinity with my own specific social outlook and practice. I have worked since 1984 with and for Kolkata's squatters and slum-dwellers, seeking to advance the rights of the city's labouring poor. Misra's stories look at the underdog and the underclass. His writing is iconoclastic and scathingly critical of social mores. So here was someone articulating, through literature and in a startlingly different way, perspectives emerging from acute social observation and reflection, and engagement with the marginalized. My make-up, outlook and work necessarily separate me from various people, even though by virtue of the multiple – often contradictory – roles I play in my life, I continue to live among them. It is therefore a lonely existence. In Misra I found a spiritual kinsman.

Subimal Misra is like a secret cult in Bengali literature.

The fact that several of Misra's stories are rooted in Kolkata and reveal the author's intimate knowledge of the city and its different strata of people also attracted me and resonated with my own make-up and engagement with my city. The vivid visualization of and topographic references to different places: the Maidan, the monument, Park Street, Khidirpur, Strand, Adi Ganga... Misra knows about the quality and character of life in the city's diverse spaces. He catches and conveys the subtle nuances of everyday life in Kolkata and Bengal through snippets of dialects of the have-nots, like the East-Bengali dialect, or the dialect of Kolkata's neighbouring district, South-24 Parganas (where many of Kolkata's labouring poor belong). Misra speaks of the quality of light and the coolness of the breeze, in a particular locale, at a particular time of the year, at a particular time of the day, in this city of Kolkata. He knows the terror that can lurk under the shadow of a tree's canopy in the Maidan.

Misra knows about the quality and character of life in the city's diverse spaces.

I have lived all my life in Kolkata, but I had not read any literature in Bengali. Subimal Misra was the first writer in Bengali whose work I actually read. While I knew about the Bengali little magazines, I was not a little-magazine reader. My relation to Bengali is as someone proficient in the language, a proficiency attained simply by living, working and socializing among

Bengali speakers. I learnt the language by ear, as someone with an urge for comprehension and sound communication. I mingle among diverse sections. As a lover of literature, I have, of course, read a fair amount, from all over the world, albeit in English, or English translation. I had done a little bit of translation into and from Bengali earlier. I liked translating; it gave me a lot of satisfaction. But I had never undertaken literary translation from Bengali to English earlier. So this was not a translator's project so much as a project's translator. In this Misra project, I saw my role as simply ferrying the stories to others through the English language.

This was not a translator's project so much as a project's translator.

For several years now, I have been studying religious texts. In this, my attitude was to implicitly accept what I was reading, without question or critique, and thus to try to understand what was written. In translating Subimal Misra, my attitude was similar: to silence any personal reactions to the writing and simply to faithfully translate the original, from my reading of what is written. Implicit in this is my insider position in this society, but I am also an outsider – a Tamilian, and ignorant about Bengali literature. That gives me an outsider's gaze, but it also limits my understanding as well as quality of translation.

In translating, my natural disposition is to be true to the original, taking no licence whatsoever. As if there is only one correct and exact translation possible! But over the years, I have learnt that there can be different ways of translating. Sometimes, the translation in English may lack the literary quality of the original; in which case, perhaps that should remain untranslated. So the main task in my translation is to get out a near-exact English version. Thereafter, I keep working on it, changing something here, cutting something there, and so on. I have also come around to the idea of taking a little licence and departing from mechanical exactitude in favour of literary quality.

Strictly speaking, a glossary or notes should accompany the stories, to provide a cultural-linguistic contextualization to the translation for the benefit of non-Bengali and non-Indian readers. A simple translation would not convey so much that each story implicitly conveys in the original – there is so much that Misra has told me: his comments on the stories, about allusions, style, and so on. But I thought that such a glossary would also make the volume rather stodgy and overbearing and, hence, that was left out.

‘ ’

I [see] my role as simply ferrying [Misra's] stories to others through the English language.

◆

I needed the comments of others, such as readers of Misra who also read in English. I shared my translations with them as well as friends and family members in Kolkata and elsewhere. I tried to follow their suggestions. Dr Mrinal Bose had not only introduced me to Subimal Misra, he had also kept after me, prodding me to begin. He enthusiastically received my translations, gave me his honest comments, critique and suggestions immediately and eagerly awaited the next story. Ankur Saha, a US-based writer and critic, and Souva Chattopadhyay, a Misra reader who wrote the Wikipedia entry on Subimal Misra and maintains a blog on Bengali parallel literature called *Boipara*, also provided much encouragement. Nilotpal Roy, a literature scholar and Misra reader, whom Misra considers to be the foremost scholar of his writing, read through the translations and made a critical evaluation. This answered some of my own doubts regarding the quality of my translation in the light of the original writing. But I remain aware of my failings. For instance, Souva asked me to write 'Brothers Whitty and Shitty' in the style of *The Canterbury Tales*. That remains to be done.

But most of all, I had the opportunity of continuing dialogue with Misra, almost entirely over the phone, which served as an education on diverse matters, as well as commentary and annotation on the stories and on his writing and thinking. I tried to internalize all this and bring to bear in my translation.

These translations are therefore, in all fairness, something like a collective project, although I take full responsibility for the final output. This is also a matter of personal satisfaction, since my own inclinations have been in the direction of the welding of individual sensibilities and energies for collective endeavours and outcomes.

◆

Dr Bose also introduced me to the name of Elfriede Jelinek, the Austrian writer who writes in German, and pointed out some similarities between Misra and Jelinek. Despite the immense difference in their backgrounds and local environments, Misra bears some resemblance to Elfriede Jelinek in making certain basic and unconventional life choices and in unflinchingly and relentlessly laying bare the rot he perceives in society. Both of them prompt these questions: What is writing? Who writes? What is written? What do we know? What do we read? Why do we read? To a reader with pretensions to writing, they prompt the question: Why do I write? Translating Misra has been a process of personal growth for me.

In real life, Subimal Misra is a simple, warm, kind-hearted, down-to-earth, gentle human being. He has no airs, no pretences, no glory, no grandeur, no renown. After over forty years of writing in anonymity, he now wears his very anonymity as a badge of honour. He is modest, but not without self-respect and respect for human dignity and independence, which he asserts with a fierce, ferocious, unstoppable vigour, notwithstanding age, dire straits, severe ill health and failing eyesight. There is an innocence, a purity and an uncorrupted quality in him. He remains an indefatigable idealist and man of principle despite the degeneration, bleakness and blight of his surroundings.

As an activist-writer, Misra is demanding. He does not give a chance to the reader to curl up comfortably with a story. That is well nigh impossible. Even understanding what exactly the author is trying to convey or achieve has to be worked at and worked out by the reader. His writing is an exercise for the reader to engage in. The comfort-seeking reader – he should pass Misra by. It would simply be a waste of time, a grievous mismatch. Misra casts his net for the appropriate reader, for the activist-reader.

As an activist-writer, Misra is demanding. He does not give a chance to the reader to curl up comfortably with a story.

Misra's anonymity and non-translation into English or any other language have meant a great loss to the Indian and world literary scene. Translating Misra is challenging, requiring time and others' critical inputs to skilfully re-render the qualities and effects of the original writing. But the translation is vital, to bring international attention to the distinctive voice and oeuvre of a gifted writer, a valiant figure in the world of literature and a ferocious thinker of the world and times we live in.

◆

Short stories form an important part of Misra's work and are also perhaps the most accessible to non-Bengali readers. Misra has written well over a hundred stories. They could more appropriately be called *prose-art* or *text-works*.

The story 'Haran Majhi's Widow's Corpse *or* the Golden Gandhi Statue' (1969) took the world of Bengali literature by storm. Portraying in a few short, staccato sentences the life of a destitute peasant family, this then became a full-blown, mythic construction, with historical, national and global connotations. The story ends, but again, not really, for the prevailing order continues to wipe out thousands of peasant families.

There is a wide variety in the subject, style and form of Misra's anti-stories. Among characteristic Misra-esque features are striking and long titles; hyper-realism; objective yet empathic depiction of the lives of marginalized people; fable-like narrative; use of folk idiom, verse and metre; reportage; cinematic techniques like montage, collage,

‘ ’

[Misra's stories] could more appropriately be called *prose-art* or *text-works*.

juxtaposition and motif; excoriating and visceral critique; and a graphic, visual and kinetic effect, akin to a movie playing inside the embedded, code-decoding consciousness of the reader to whom the work is addressed.

Misra forsakes all the rules of grammar and composition. His stories are often long, barely punctuated narratives – continuous, unrelenting, unsparing – written in that form simply to assail the reader, to bring him to the point of suffocating distress.

Misra has written about assaulting the middle-class consciousness. Hence, some people might consider Misra's stories to be gruesome or revolting.

Misra has written about assaulting the middle-class consciousness. Hence, some people might consider Misra's stories to be gruesome or revolting.

In Misra's prose compilation *Son and Murderer* (1996), the acclaimed Bengali writer Debesh Ray acknowledges that Misra has given a special form to postmodern discourse in Bengali literature. He says, 'Subimal Misra could easily have written good stories in the conventional sense. Instead, he chose to make the story-writing itself the subject of the story. He hasn't confined himself to the limits of form. As a result of his personal choices, his stories, rather than being called stories, could also be called prose.'

A microscopic observer of people and society (like the Urdu writer Manto), he is a sociologist of spoken Bengali, with a keen ear for the language, accents and intonations of common folk, street argot full of slang and vulgarity, as well as the vainglorious puerilities of the middle class. He often cocks a snook at and makes mischief with the niceties of spelling, syntax, punctuation and composition.

Gandhi, the father of the Indian nation, appears in some of Misra's stories. In this collection, 'The Golden Gandhi Statue from America', 'Brothers Whitty and Shitty' and 'Money Tree' refer to Gandhi. Gandhi's statue is a central element in the first story. It falls and breaks during a bout of political agitation and America promises to replace it with a golden one. The Gandhi-cap-clad criminal-politician in 'Brothers…' counsels the failed rail wagon thieves to be Gandhi-like in their profession, mirroring the state of what the very name of the father of the nation has come to signify. Very close to the site of the toppled Gandhi statue lies the dead white donkey in 'Money Tree'. Misra had told me that the white donkey symbolized Gandhi. Another of Misra's Gandhi stories is 'Mohandas o Aenr Kata' ('Mohandas and the One-balled Man', 1986). In this, a man who loses one of his testicles in a bizarre accident ekes out a living by impersonating Gandhi and standing statue-like in public places. He finds it increasingly difficult to survive and contemplates going to Bengal, where he thinks the new Leftist government might give him a job.

> [Misra] often cocks a snook at and makes mischief with the niceties of spelling, syntax, punctuation and composition.

## Books by Subimal Misra

***Stories***

*Haran Majhir Bidhoba Bouer Mora ba Shonar Gandhimurti*
(Haran Majhi's Widow's Corpse or the Golden Gandhi Statue)

*Nanga Haar Jegey Uthchhey*
(Bare Bones Awakened)

*Dui Tin-te Udom Bachcha Chhutochhuti Korchey Level Crossing-e Borabor*
(Two or Three Naked Children Run Around Beside the Level Crossing)

*Bobby*

*Aar Pipegun Eto Gorom Hoye Jaay Je Er Byabohar Krumosho Komey Ashchhey*
(And the Pipegun Gets So Hot That Its Use Is Steadily Reduced)

*Shreshto Golpo*
(Selected Stories)

*Ei Amader Shiki Lebu Ningrani*

Subimal Misra's stories must be read over and over again, and one should think about them whenever possible. By and by, they grow on you, or in you. You find things around you echoing characters, images and words from his stories. After the devastating fire in March 2010 at Stephen Court in Kolkata's Park Street, reports and images in city newspapers seemed to come out of Misra's stories of nearly four decades ago: the pervasive stench of death, vultures sitting on rooftops in the heart of the city, an old man muttering that he is searching for his dead son's bones... The dire warning in 'The Golden Gandhi Statue from America' – *The one who will vanquish you is thriving in Gokul* – in the light of the Maoist insurgency in West Bengal in 2010, Jangalmahal becomes the mythic Gokul. And the psychographies of extremist youth in Misra's stories from the 1960s Naxalite era, such as 'Blood', 'The Dagger' and 'Feeling Distant', can also be re-read in the context of the current Maoist upsurge in various parts of India.

In an interview, Misra said of his writing: 'I don't want to write anything which makes people pat me on my back and say, "Well done, this is great literature boy!" I want people to read my writing and spit on my face, to point at me and say, "Here's the one who pokes and pricks the wounds of this syphilitic civilization and reveals them like the clear light of day."' In *Bobby* (1985), he wrote, 'I believe in carrying out a kind of "planned violence" through my writing.' Misra's stories document in depth the land of Bengal in the last three decades of the twentieth century. He writes of its marginalized people, its degeneration, hungers, lusts and hyper-violent reality. As critic Ankur Saha writes in an article on Misra in the Bengali literary e-zine *Parabaas*, 'In contemporary Bengali literature, no one calls a spade a spade as boldly as Subimal Misra does.'

◆

Since Misra's linguistic-sensory-cognitive-cerebral universe is immediately and primarily Bengali and Kolkata-based, in a very specific way, his writing is therefore fundamentally untranslatable – in the sense that the lived experience within a specific historical-cultural-social-intellectual-institutional-canonical system shall necessarily remain unknown to a reader in a manner that the best of glossaries and annotations cannot aid.

Misra's writing is deeply Bengali. But he is simultaneously locally rooted and universal. Though deeply embedded in the vernacular Bengali world, his writing is informed about current affairs and inspired by world literature. His humane vision emanates from a corporeal engagement with the world around us – as a human being, identical in so many ways to

**Books**

(This Is How We Squeeze a Quarter of Lemon)

*Anti-Golpo Sangroho* (Anti-Stories Collection)

*Satyo Utpadityo Hoy* (Truth Is Manufactured)

*Kaath Khay Aangra Haagey* (Wood Eats, Charcoal Shits)

*Chhottrish Bochorer Rograrogri* (Thirty-six Years' Scuffles)

*Kika Cut-out*

*Premer Mora Joley Dobey Na* (Cupid's Corpse Does Not Drown in Water)

*Haatey Dhoriye Deowa Hoyeche Shesh-Hobishyir Maalshabhog – Aar, Ebong, Haashtey Haashtey, Khorkutor Moto Bheshey Jaowar Anando-Gourob* (The Pot of Sacred Rice – Funerary Rites Completed, Blissful Pride)

any human being anywhere, but depicted in shades, tones, accents, strokes and sounds that are purely and incommunicably local and Bengali.

Notwithstanding this specificity, the wider relevance of Misra's writing lies in its engagement with what are also, ultimately, fundamental questions confronting all of humanity—all societies, nations, governments and every human being. These are seen in the raw as it were – exposed, uncovered, naked – in Kolkata. Hence, the local specificity is also a means whereby the globally relevant art and text product is imbued with a powerful, well-rounded, integral, throbbing, buzzing rawness and immediacy. As if the heart of feeble humanity is itself pulsating in the reader's palm.

That local and corporeal specificity is thus testimony to the minute observer of human life that Misra is; to the activist that he is, a toiler for a future that is of better taste, where the real life of literature can begin, in a hitherto predominantly unlettered society.

But illiteracy is also a metaphor for the comatose, zombie-like, media-fed and consumption-fed existence that postmodern, global, capitalist economy-society-culture has produced. An order which denies the possibility of the human being exercising himself or herself as a complete, free, aware, tasteful, ethical entity rather than a mindless,

## Books

***Novels***

*Tejoskriyo Aborjona*
(Radioactive Waste)

*Asholey Eti Ramayan Chamarer Golpo Hoye Uthtey Parto*
(Actually This Could Have Become Ramayan Chamar's Story)

*Rong Jokhon Sotorkikoroner Chinnhho*
(When Colour is the Symbol of Danger)

*Kontho Palok Ora – Shobkichui Ba Bajaar Cholito Bastobotagulike Obishyashjogyo Korey Tolar Koushal*
(The Feathered Neck – Everything, or the Knack of Rendering the Marketable Realities Unbelievable)

*Aadyonto Manush*
(Complete Man)

*Anti-Uponyash Songroho*
(Anti-Novels Collection)

manipulated, herd-driven, lust-fulfilling animal.

There may never be dignity and justice for all in this planet. The poor are perhaps too powerless and the powerful who matter and who can effect change are too caught up in their own vain pursuits to look beyond themselves… So Misra does not give in to despair or frustration. He lauds the acts of subversion and rebellion by the oppressed as the only moments of celebration in this bleak, hopeless life.

Misra believes that the world would be far more beautiful when many more voices are unleashed. In that yet-to-come world, dalit writers will write about the dalit reality of dalits and find international renown, the landless peasant Haran Majhi will read and write. But until then, the best response to the current world order may be something like the image Misra concludes his story 'Dui Tin-te Udom Bachcha…' ('Two or Three Naked Children…') with, an image that one can easily find in Kolkata: a naked, prancing urchin, gleefully mocking the world passing him by, clutching his genitals and parodying the Hindi film song: 'Bol, Radha, bol, sangam hoga ki nahin…'

Subimal Misra's relevance in the world of literature is that he has shown how to assail and demolish the prevailing order as a writer, in his time and place, doing all he

## Books

*One Pice Father Mother* (A Penny's My Father and Mother)

*Chetey Chushey Chibiye Giley* (Lick, Suck, Munch, Gulp)

***Essays***

*Subimaler Biruddhe Subimal Ebong Ushkanimulok Onek Kichui Aapaat Bhabey* (Subimal Against Subimal and a Lot of Apparently Exciting Things)

*Lohar Taar Baagh o Dorshoker Modhye Rokto Bhalobhashey* (Between the Tiger and the Spectator, the Barbed Wire Loves Blood)

*Son and Murderer*

*Taamaaker Baajaar Bonam Euclider Chotushparsho Ebong Aro Aro Paaltikhaowa Ebong Aro Aro Ushkanimulok* (The Tobacco Market Versus Euclid's possibly can. And he has done this on and on, ever more penetratingly, even as he himself became ever more marginalized. But he thus managed to keep the candle of hope of an alternative flickering in the face of the all-enveloping darkness of an arrogant, commercial singularity.

## Books

Environs and Plenty of Turnarounds and Plenty of Excitement)

***Play***

*Bhaitu Paathaar Ishtu*
(Brother Goat's Stew)

***Graphical Text-works***

*Haar Mormori*
(Clatter of Bones)

*Guer Pnod Teen Jaaygaay Laagey*
(The Shitty Bum Touches Three Places)

## On This Translation

'V. Ramaswamy knows the city of Kolkata as few others of his background do; he has worked intimately with its urban planning and in connection to its poorer habitations and settlements for years. In this regard, his choice of the reputed experimental writer Subimal Misra for translation is apposite – given Misra's unflinching but mischievous gaze, his eye roving the more ragged thoroughfares of this city – and perhaps an extension of Ramaswamy's deep search for a way of living without disillusionment, but also without illusions, in Kolkata. Ramaswamy has himself written, with great eloquence and knowledge, of the contingencies of existence in this city; and, in translating Misra, I think he has given a significant writer – as well as an extraordinary phase in Bengali literature (responding as it was to the upheavals of Maoist politics in a traumatized Bengal in the late sixties) – a new lease of life. I think he has found a language in these translations that is at once meticulously crafted and fluid – an urgent poetic vernacular suited well to Misra's nightmarish but lyrical world, a diction at once fresh, urgent and readable. The Bengali language, with its remarkable storehouse of achievements, badly needs translators of excellence; in Ramaswamy, it has one. We can expect a great deal more from him.'

– Amit Chaudhuri

'For those of us who grew up in the rich literary forests of what are called 'vernacular' Indian languages, it has always been a source of great pain to see wonderful works fall into the troughs of execrable translation before it can reach a wider trans-national and international readership. This curse has so blighted the different 'bhasha' literatures that often it seems better for a work to remain outside the massive tent of English text than be traduced and trampled just inside its periphery. V. Ramaswamy is one of the few exceptions working in India today – a translator who gives me hope. His understanding of Bengali culture has been deeply honed by years of dynamic interaction with Kolkata and Bengal. Alongside this understanding is an uncanny ability to grasp the inner cadences of different kinds of Bangla as well as the skill and courage that all really brilliant translators need to have vis-à-vis the language into which they are translating – in this case, English.

V. Ramaswamy's translations of the Bangla master Subimal Misra's short stories will, I'm certain, be regarded as a breakthrough in the world of Indian letters. Misra, a path-breaking modernist pushing the boundaries of both form and language, has for too long been kept from a discerning non-Bengali readership. He has now found in V. Ramaswamy an inspired partner to help his writing make the leap to English. It is, I hope, the beginning of a long and fruitful partnership between this translator and his chosen original language, a partnership that will show the way for other translators working in other Indian languages.'

– Ruchir Joshi